CHRISSY HOPEWELL

 Created with Vellum

ALSO BY CHRISSY HOPEWELL

If We Pretend

Unless It's You

Since We're Here

One Hundred Lights (holiday novella)

Sign up to Chrissy's newsletter for extra content, including bonus scenes for every novel.

www.ChrissyHopewell.com

1

BRITT

Monday, December 11

I wouldn't call myself the protagonist of this story. That sounds far too positive. More like the slightly-morally-gray main character. I've tried, I really have.

A year ago, Reese and I drank Baileys at this table, partaking in our annual best friend tradition of watching cheesy holiday rom-coms on Netflix, picking out the obvious plot holes and making fun of the performances from previously famous actors. I wrapped presents, overdoing it as usual for both my son, Jackson, and Reese's family, and she ordered last minute presents online. It was perfect.

But this year, it's just me watching movies, focusing even more on making things magical for Jackson. The holidays will be completely different without the tradition of sharing Christmas Eve with Reese's family.

And it's my own damn fault.

"Captain, don't you dare." I shake my head at the gray tuxedo cat who's waving his paw next to my glass of red wine. If he had eyebrows, he'd be raising them. If he could talk, he'd say something like, *I'm in charge here, and don't you freaking forget it.* I slowly stand and inch my hand closer.

He raises his paw higher, increasing the threat.

"Captain Underpants. I beg of you."

Usually, I prefer to not call this cat by the full name he was given two years ago by my son. Never trust a ten-year-old child to name your pets. Jackson named our other cat Vanilla Frappuccino, Frappy for short. Could be worse, but I suspect the poor animal is self conscious because he's mortified at being named after a Starbucks drink.

Captain Underpants has no such insecurities.

Captain opens his mouth for a soundless meow. I'd read cats only meow at humans, not each other. I meow back. We stare at each other, his paw still raised in the air, me giving him my most authoritative glare. I lunge for the wineglass. He leaps off the table, walking away with his tail straight up.

I let out an amused snort and sip deeply, letting the liquid warm my throat and belly.

Damn. I'm going to need a new pet sitter next month when I go away to pitch to one of the Silicon Valley venture capitalists with the tech start-up I'm currently hosting in the Idea Garage, the converted team space attached to my house. I haven't traveled since I screwed up my best friendship.

I breathe in through my nose and hold it for a second before letting the air slowly out of my mouth. Six months ago, I thought I was doing the right thing. It was my problem, not theirs—my inappropriate, unwelcome feelings for Reese's husband, Adrian.

I felt awful about it.

That was why I'd decided to take a break from spending so much time with them. We just needed some time apart. Especially after she'd confessed to me at a women's retreat that she was having marital problems.

But when I told her I needed space, she saw right through me, the betrayal immediately sinking in.

Losing pet sitters you can trust with your garage code is bad, but it's not even near the top of the list of things that suck about this situation. My stomach twists at the painful memory of running into Adrian at the high school musical a few weeks ago. I'd literally dropped to the floor and rolled behind a group of parents, as if I was on fire.

And Adrian saw me do it.

A buzz on the table distracts me from the humiliating memory. I search for my phone from among the piles of wrapped presents. The text might be from the PTO president about this Friday's holiday dance. The parent running the event is sick and I got an email a few hours ago begging someone to take over. I should have said, *No thank you! Enough on my plate!* But I feel bad enough for everything that's happened this year. I could use all the help I could get to return to some kind of karmic balance.

I really, really want Jackson to have a great time at the dance. A magical time, even. If that means I need to sacrifice this week to make sure of it, then I'll do it.

When I was a kid, the holidays were cold and boring. Half the time my parents were off traveling somewhere exotic, usually leaving me and my older brother with au pairs. It was lonely in our quiet house, knowing our friends' houses were full of holiday joy. And Jackson must miss Adrian and Reese's daughter, Chelsea. Middle school has been hard enough for him, but now, thanks to me, he's lost one of his best friends too.

Where the hell is my phone? Ah. I find it behind a wrapped stack of six identical portable phone chargers, tied with curled ribbon, ready to hand out to my team.

A text from my friend Laura lights up the screen.

LAURA

Adrian's here at CrossFit. Asking about you.
Again

I suck air in, my insides knotting at the thought of Adrian

hanging out at the gym, the place where we spent so much time together. I still miss him and his boring stories about work as a financial advisor, or the wordless way we communicated through facial expressions, making fun of some beefcake working out next to us.

Scrolling up, I re-read the texts Laura sent me last week, where Adrian told her that his divorce was final.

I caused that divorce. First, showing up at Reese's doorstep. When that went badly, I headed to the airport to intercept Adrian. He'd looked delighted to see me at first, if not confused. I can still feel his arms wrapping around my waist after he dropped his bags. Letting me come closer than was appropriate. When I told him I needed space, that Reese was my best friend . . . his face changed. More confusion.

Then something else.

I didn't see reciprocated feelings, that was for sure. But I didn't want that. I was trying to avoid it by pushing them away. I should have just silently kept my feelings to myself, done what my parents did—locked them in a safe and forgot the code. The one fight I heard my parents have when I was a teenager—a whispered argument I eavesdropped on through our shared bedroom wall—was about my father cheating. My world shook—the floor felt like jelly beneath my knees. My father, so boring and unemotional, had had an affair? But they barely talked about it. Mom asked him if it had ended. He said yes. That was it.

I don't want to live like that. I don't want to be a home wrecker, either. I'd been on the receiving end of that kind of behavior before.

My ex-husband continued to work late hours in New York City long after we moved to the Jersey suburbs, and he spent those late nights and midnight takeouts with his coworker.

He should have seen it coming and stopped it. Only he didn't.

She fell for him, and then they started sleeping together.

And then he fell for her.

After our divorce, I swore I'd always be open and honest with myself and those around me. Even knowing all that, I'd screwed up and lost both my best friends at once.

And now I've successfully avoided Adrian and Reese for six months. Neither of them seems to mind. The empty pit of loneliness inside me contracts, longing for a ray of hope in Laura's text message.

ME

What'd he say?

LAURA

Like last week, he asked if I'd seen you. This time, he asked how you are. If you ever work out anymore. It's the most he's ever said to me. And possibly the most awkward conversation I've had in my life

I swallow and close my eyes. Adrian was anything but awkward with me.

ME

What'd you tell him?

LAURA

That you're doing just fine. What'd you want me to say?

ME

Nothing

LAURA

Want me to go punch him in the nuts? Or maybe let my hand linger on his body while I 'spot' him? I can pretend to be you from seven months ago. You two were always touching each other

ME

Were we?

> LAURA
>
> Hello? Yes. Married or not, it was constant.

Oh, no. The inappropriate feelings? My fault. The divorce? Also, my fault. Confirmed.

When I reconnected with Adrian, my older brother's childhood friend, six years ago, I had no idea he and his wife would become our closest friends in town. It was innocent.

There was that one kiss Adrian and I shared after I graduated high school so long ago, before he got together with Reese. My brother had a party one night when my parents were away, and I ended up in a dark corner with Adrian, who had had a few drinks and was incredibly flirty. But my brother freaked out when he found out, and Adrian never crossed that line again, no matter how much I wanted him to.

It was ancient history.

I never did tell Reese about that kiss, and I assume Adrian didn't either. There was nothing to tell.

Reese and I were immediate besties. We had the same taste in clothes, loved the same movies, laughed at the same cheesy jokes, and were both obsessed with our cranky cats. She helped me through the divorce, immediately taking my side like a protective older sister.

But now she'll probably never talk to me again.

I miss both of them.

And I miss working out. I massage my biceps. Have they become softer? Shit. I need another way to stay in shape.

I get up and move to the long sectional couch, grabbing my laptop from the coffee table before settling in. The Idea Garage will be open this week, then shut for the last two weeks of the year. I bought this house because it had a one-car garage attached to the house, plus a giant garage next to it, which I converted to a working space complete with a kitchen, bathroom, large open area with multiple tables, plus a cozy loft with bean bags and two more small, mismatched tables I found at an estate sale.

I got lucky. Walking away from my divorce with some money, I'd used my corporate experience and the MBA I got when Jackson was young to invest in a few app startups, giving them my coaching and input. As it turns out, I have a knack for that kind of thing. So when we sold the first app—a corporate training video game—I officially started the Idea Garage, hosting one team at a time. My place is within easy access to New York City and offers meeting space, funding, and coaching, in exchange for a cut of the profits when the apps sell. I'm always trying to make it better. The team currently rents a house across town, but when something comes up around here, I'll buy it and convert it into team living quarters.

Do I spoil the twenty-something-year-old teams with gifts and affection, as well as strategic guidance and management? Yes. Yes, I do.

I settle down and Frappy, my giant white snowball of a cat, materializes out of nowhere and settles on my lap, so I balance my laptop on the arm of the couch. There are zero responses to the post I made on the parent message board an hour ago about an emergency school dance meeting tomorrow night at my house.

"Shit."

Frappy looks at me with her yellow eyes, unimpressed with my concern or obsession with making the holidays perfect.

I get that everyone is busy at this time of year, but I'm hoping a few parents will help finalize the details for Friday's event. I'm not sure what the chair was doing before she got sick, because the decorations are buried in some storage closet in the school basement, status unknown, the chaperone list isn't finalized (or even started, maybe?), and I know nothing about the catering. I need a handful of good volunteers.

Making the school dance amazing shouldn't be that hard. Maybe it won't solve the ache in my heart from losing Adrian and Reese, but it'll show Jackson that I would do anything for him.

2

ADRIAN

Laura walks away, our short, unhelpful conversation finished. The sliver of hope that formed in my belly when I saw Britt's gym friend disappears.

"Dammit." I stretch out my shoulders by pulling my left arm across my body and gently pushing my elbow.

When I started coming back to CrossFit two weeks ago, did I expect Britt would be waiting for me by the medicine balls, eyes filled with tears, ready to restart our friendship? Maybe. I'd rotated my days to see if maybe I was just missing her, but now I know.

Britt hasn't returned since that night at the airport.

And the look she gave me at the high school musical two weeks ago?

Ouch.

I was waiting in the lobby for Chelsea, which, in hindsight, wasn't my best idea. What teenager wants their parent waiting for them like that? I'm still figuring out how to be a single dad. Trying to let Chelsea know she's the most important person in the world to me.

Britt walked out of the auditorium with Jackson and one of his friends. She screeched to a halt, eyes wide like a baby deer's in the beams of a tractor trailer, and disappeared behind a group of parents. If I didn't know better, I'd swear she actually dropped to the floor. But it got crowded right afterward and I couldn't spot her again.

I know one thing—it can't go on like this.

A beefy dude grunts, lifting the deadlift bar in front of me as his giant muscles strain against his skin. The sharp, unpleasant scent of end-of-workout body odor drifts over. I take a step back to save my senses, stretching my right shoulder.

I shouldn't have let us go so long without talking. Not after how things happened. I almost texted her a hundred times. Called her, stopped by her house or the Idea Garage, where our families had spent so much time together over the past six years.

But things were complicated with Reese.

After Britt announced she was stepping away from us, I'd thought more about my marriage, diving in with my therapist, separate from the marriage counseling Reese and I'd been attending. But it was too late. Too many years of distance and our connection was permanently gone. When Chelsea got to middle school and was suddenly even busier than before with soccer and a newfound social life, Reese and I found ourselves staring at each other as strangers.

We tried, but our marriage was over. I moved out a few weeks later.

So we didn't get divorced because of Britt.

But then again, we also kind of did.

It took me a while to realize how much I missed Britt. As a friend. I just have to be careful how I do this. Britt walked away from me then, and I let her go.

Of course I did. I was married. She was one of our best friends.

After growing up with parents who loved fiercely, fought wildly, and cheated without abandon before divorcing, I'd always wanted to provide the most stable, quiet, and even boring life for myself and my family.

Clearly, I fucked that up, taking it too far in the other direction in my marriage. I was too detached. Too unemotional.

Beefy dude walks away and I take his place in front of the barbells, removing one weight, two weights, okay, five more weights before starting my lifts. Keeping my back straight, I squat to grab the barbell, then push up hard until I'm standing with locked knees. I do four sets of five reps until my whole body is screaming.

Across the room, Laura taps at her phone by the front door, slipping on her winter jacket. She glances up and looks directly at me as she disappears into the winter evening. I clench my fists and curse under my breath.

My muscles aching, I stretch against a wall, pulling my quads one at a time, then reaching down to touch the floor, feeling a satisfying burn in my calves.

All my intentions of keeping my family life stable to counteract the one I had growing up were gone. I'd already failed Chelsea.

And now I can't stop thinking about Britt. I need to talk to her. Smooth things over.

I miss her.

That means nothing except that we were close friends. I want to see her face again. Close up—not as she dives away from me at a school event.

I've never been so trapped in my head. I feel like our cat—Reese's cat—must have felt when it got locked in the pantry for an entire workday. He was furious with us when we finally got home.

But at least he escaped. I'm still locked in that closet.

At my locker, I pull on my hooded sweatshirt and grab my keys and phone, letting the face ID unlock my screen and clicking through to my email by habit.

A message from Britt is at the top of my inbox.

My pulse races before I realize it's an automated email from a school message board, not personally sent to me. Now that I'm running solo, I signed up for all the email notifications from school. There are so many emails asking for donations or volunteers or reminders about themed days or standardized testing. Why do high schoolers still have pajama days?

I didn't realize how much Reese had been doing all these years. I let out a rush of air and click the message.

To: All Parents
Subject: Urgent Winter Dance Volunteer Meeting

Hi Everyone,

I'm your new Winter Dance chair because Vicky had to step down. There will be an urgent volunteer meeting tomorrow (Tuesday) evening at my house at seven o'clock. I need some help to wrap things up and make the night magical for our children!

Let me know if you can come.

Thank you, Britt

A smile creeps on my face. It's so Britt to volunteer to chair the dance last minute. I wonder if she's wrapping gifts for each student, or personally monogramming backpacks. Britt's an incredibly thoughtful gift-giver. Last year, she bought Reese a stack of international travel guidebooks—actual, physical copies with gorgeous color posters—because Reese had mentioned going to Scotland or Europe with Chelsea. And she'd ordered a half dozen bags of my favorite coffee beans from the Jersey Shore, where we'd all rented a house together two summers ago.

Thinking about it now, I see how Britt had integrated so deeply into our lives. Our marriage. But it felt natural, as if she was an extended family member.

And last year, we'd all signed up for CrossFit together. Reese bailed at the last minute when she threw out her back, and never did join us. And then, it had just been the two of us. Me and Britt. Too much time spent together. Too many days we'd gone for a drink afterward and laughed and talked and let our bond grow.

Shit. Why'd we do that?

If I were a better person, I would have seen it happening. I would have stopped it.

But I didn't. When I had to spot her doing presses at the gym, maybe I'd let a hand linger on her skin. Maybe I'd gazed into her eyes for too long across a table. We never crossed the line physically, not since that innocent kiss decades ago, but I can't deny my attraction to her had grown over time, even though I hadn't realized it.

But if it was just a simple attraction, wouldn't it be gone by now? Maybe it is. Besides smoothing things over between us, I need to know how I feel when I see Britt again.

She's avoided me for so long, but I know where she'll be tomorrow night. I can show up to the Idea Garage and she won't be able to run. And I can do this without messing up things with Chelsea, right?

I squint my eyes shut and picture Britt's face. She's beautiful. Deep-blue eyes surrounded by dark lashes, light blond hair she usually wears in a braid or a thick high ponytail. Her smile is sweet and subtle, her laugh loud and contagious.

I miss the sound.

The cold December air slices into my skin as I head out of CrossFit and through the parking lot to my car.

I still don't know what I feel for Britt. But I need to find out.

3

BRITT

Tuesday, December 12

Only four volunteers have showed up so far, and most of them are terrifying, cliquey PTO moms. Is no one else interested in making this dance magical for their children? Maybe four is enough, especially given that one already messaged me saying three of them volunteered last year and would stop by the school on their way to assess decorations in the storage closet.

"Let's just give everyone else two more minutes, okay? Anyone want coffee?" I'm lingering in the kitchen while the trio of moms get cozy on the couch, obviously close friends. I vaguely recognize them from previous school events. They are all clutching large Starbucks cups. Another mom, dressed in business casual and with curled hair and full makeup, is staring at her phone at the table where I wrapped presents last night.

The dark-haired mom with a red infinity scarf glances up and gestures to her coffee.

"We're good." Then she goes back to her conversation with the other women.

Must be nice. I'm betting none of them developed inappropriate feelings for the other's husband. Or at least if they did, they knew better than to say anything about it.

A calendar notification pops up on my phone. It's seven o'clock.

"Okay! Let's get started." I move awkwardly to the front of the couch, feeling like I'm about to give a formal presentation. I back up and sit on the single couch chair, facing away from the outside door to the Idea Garage.

"Tell me more later," the mom with a cute blond bob whispers loudly to a woman with a gray ponytail.

"I appreciate you all joining me at the last minute. As you know, Vicky's out of commission, so I'm just trying to wrap things up for Friday's dance."

"We swung by the school on the way here," cute blond bob mom says. "I'm Liz, by the way."

"I'm Sara," red infinity scarf mom chirps.

"Jill." Jill swings her gray ponytail and waggles her fingers at me.

Corporate mom pipes in, introducing herself as Grace, barely looking up from whatever she's been furiously tapping away at on her phone.

"Hi. And awesome. Thank you. I hadn't even figured out how to get the key to the storage closet."

"There's no key. You just have to be brave enough to descend into the high school basement," Sara says, and the other moms on the couch giggle.

"That feels like a bad idea." Grace crinkles her forehead.

"Kinda does." I don't even know where the basement is, given that Jackson goes to classes across the street in the middle school. "Is everything we need in there?"

"Well. Good news and bad news—" Liz stops talking when a click at the front door distracts her.

I turn my head and a squeak escapes my throat, loud enough

that I sense the women glancing at me, instead of the man standing in the doorframe.

It's Adrian, and the sight of him takes my breath away.

Towering there on the welcome mat with freshly cut dark hair that swoops onto his forehead and two-day stubble, he's everything I've ever wanted . . . but couldn't have.

And he's staring right at me with brown, broody, intense eyes, like there's not a room of PTO moms.

"Sorry I'm late." Adrian slips his jacket off.

Waving my hand toward corporate mom Grace, where there's an empty chair, I attempt to do normal things with my mouth.

"Thanks for coming." My voice comes out scratchy and soft, as if we're somewhere else—perhaps all alone under romantic moonlight and shooting stars and he's about to confess his love—not in my house with a bunch of moms. A ridiculous thought.

But I can't stop staring.

Why *is* he here? To volunteer for the school dance? That doesn't feel like something Adrian would do. That was always Reese's thing, taking care of all of Chelsea's school stuff and juggling her job, while Adrian focused solely on work.

And CrossFit, eventually.

Gray ponytail mom—otherwise known as Jill—clears her throat. I whip my attention away from Adrian back to the couch o' scary PTO moms.

"What were we talking about?" I'm totally thrown off my game.

"Storage closet," Jill says, eyebrows raised.

"Right. Good news and bad news. Go on." I focus on her, then back to Liz as she takes a breath to talk.

"The good news is *most* of the winter dance decorations were in plastic bins."

"Excellent." I nod my head enthusiastically, all too aware of Adrian's eyes on me. All these months of me running from him and Reese, avoiding talking to or being anywhere close to them, and now he's in my house. He shouldn't be here.

Nausea crashes over me and I clench my stomach muscles, trying to dissipate the feeling. Or is that an excited fluttering? The negative and positive are entwined together, impossible to detangle.

"Oh." My brain re-plays Liz's sentence. "Most? So what's the bad news?"

"Everything was stored in that wet, nasty closet. There was a leak that ruined all of the strands of pretty white lights." She makes a face.

"All of them? Oh, shit."

"Yeah. Someone haphazardly stored them in cardboard boxes. I'm not sure who was on the cleanup crew last year, but they really screwed up. We dragged them behind the school to the dumpster."

"So we have no lights at all for our winter dance?"

"Correct. And we ran to Target on the way here, but the store is totally sold out. Then we had to get to this meeting, so . . ." She sips from her coffee, daring me to question whether they could have looked at another store instead of getting Starbucks.

"Oh my god." This is going to be an enormous problem. Lights are the cornerstone of any good holiday decor. Without lights, the dance will be dark and boring. It won't be festive at all.

Just like Christmas Eve without Adrian.

Or Reese and Chelsea. Jackson, too, since he'll be with his father for the first time in years. "Okay, let's get through the other things first, then I can think about lights."

"Someone should probably report the leak to school maintenance." Liz looks pointedly at me.

"Yes, yes, of course." I realize they mean me. The school dance chair. "I'll take care of that." I add it to the to-do list I've started.

"As for other responsibilities," Liz continues, "Sara and I were already coordinating the food. That's all under control, so we just have a few follow-ups this week."

I thought someone said Vicky had *everything* under control. I guess that wasn't quite right.

"Did you hear from the caterer this afternoon?" Sara turns toward her friend.

"Yup, let me find the email." Liz scrolls on her phone.

I sneak a look over at Adrian, who hasn't said a word. He's watching me. Waiting for me to make eye contact. An electric current crackles between us. There's so much unsaid, so many stories left to tell . . . so much that I ruined with my dumb confession about my stupid feelings.

His lips curl up in a small smile and he mouths: *hey.*

My eyes grow wide and old butterflies rise from the dead in my stomach. What's happening here? I look away quickly as Liz updates us all on what the caterer said.

Thirty minutes later, we've established Jill will coordinate the setup and cleanup volunteers, Grace will follow up with the DJ, and I'll manage the main chaperone list, which Vicky thankfully *had* started in a Google Doc.

"Finally, the lights, I guess," I say. "I can find new ones. I have a few days, maybe I can order them online or something . . ." A gym full of fairy lights by Friday, two weeks before Christmas? Still, I have to make it happen. After school yesterday, I told Jackson I was in charge of the dance and his eyes lit up, a big smile on his face.

"Yeah. You'll probably need a hundred boxes." Liz raises her eyebrows. "Literally."

A hundred boxes? Sounds like a holiday nightmare. Crowded stores, empty shelves, grumpy employees.

"I'll help you." Everyone's head whips around to Adrian, except mine, which rotates in super slow motion. He hasn't added a word to the conversation. I bet the other moms forgot he was even there.

I didn't, though.

"You'll help me?" My voice does not sound normal. My eyes

dart to the moms on the couch, who are all watching us interact, eyes wide and interested.

"Yes. I can help you find lights. For the dance?"

One mom giggles. No clue which one.

I swallow a lump that appears in my throat, threatening to choke me.

Why would he volunteer for this? It's bad enough he's here, in my house, looking the way he does, making me feel things I've been trying to beat down for the past six months. But now he wants to spend extra time together this week? One on one?

I can't do this. What would we even talk about? What if I say something stupid again? What if Reese finds out? I want to talk to her at some point. Apologize. Beg for her friendship. I've been desperately lonely. I need my best friend back.

Only what if she finds out about me and Adrian going on this light-hunting expedition?

But that isn't my greatest fear, not right now.

My greatest fear is this: what if I find out that my inappropriate feelings for Adrian are still raging? That me removing myself from the situation not only screwed up their marriage, but didn't do what I'd intended? It would mean I'm like my ex-husband's new wife, who let herself fall for a married man.

I hate that I broke my best friend's marriage.

"You might need to run to a bunch of stores to find enough lights. I'll help. Okay, Britt?" His voice is steady, as if he's trying to calm a freaked-out child or an anxious cat. I feel like a little of both.

"Great. Thank you." I practically bark the words to sound confident and normal. Sara flinches dramatically. Jill snort-laughs.

Perfect. The PTO moms think I'm a freak show.

The meeting wraps and the four moms jet out of the Idea Garage, promising to connect within the next day, leaving me standing by the door with it cracked open. Adrian remains seated at the table. He hasn't moved.

I turn, but feeling half like crying and half like hysterically laughing, I can't bring myself to make eye contact with him. I want to run over and throw my arms around his neck, but I also want to stand here like a statue until he leaves me in peace.

Adrian is untouchable.

We can't work together to find one hundred boxes of lights.

If I keep doing things wrong in life, I'll never find what I'm looking for, whatever or whoever that is.

I'll never be happy.

"Britt. Look at me."

The moms' cars are gone. The house is quiet.

I'll just tell Adrian I don't need his help.

All I have to do is find the nerve to face him.

4

ADRIAN

She finally turns around, and the look on her face almost breaks me.

It's not the raw, naked, open look she gave me when I first walked in, before she remembered who I am and the reasons I shouldn't be here. Her forehead crinkles, her lips press together, and her eyes squint.

Oh, fuck me, is she about to cry?

I should leave her alone. She doesn't want me here. Britt stepped away from me six months ago and I don't think anything has changed for her. She doesn't want to pursue me. Hell, she probably managed to completely kill whatever feelings she had for me.

But Jesus, it's good to see her face and look into her dark-blue eyes. Mine trace the curve of her jaw and the slope of her long neck. She's wearing a wide-necked white sweater that's falling off one shoulder, exposing a white lace bra strap. Her thick, light-blond braid rests in the crook of her neck. I picture myself burying my face in that space, and the vision ignites inside of me like a lit match thrown at a dry pile of leaves.

Damn. That's something I should not be thinking about.

"You should go." Her voice is unsteady, hands clasped together, door still open and letting cold air spill in. "The meeting's over."

I breathe in to respond, but what do I say? I don't want to leave yet?

"I want to help," I say instead. "I'm, uh, trying to get more involved in things since the divorce."

She flinches at the word and crosses her arms over her chest.

"Reese handled everything with Chelsea and the school. It's kind of overwhelming."

Her eyebrows lift, but she stays silent.

"Do you know what it's like to try to get in with all those moms?" I nod my head toward the empty driveway. "They are so judgmental. I could use some tips on how to break in. And that online homework system? For fuck's sake, that's impossible to understand."

The words pour out of me. I am trying hard for Chelsea, but it never feels like enough.

The corner of her mouth quirks, but she doesn't let the smile form.

"I don't know how to break into the PTO mom circle either," she says. "So I'm not sure I can help you."

"Britt." I sigh. "I want to be a good dad." My voice cracks at the end.

"You are," she murmurs, her face softening. "Just worrying about that stuff means you are."

I shake my head, stand, and approach her. She takes a visible breath, her shoulders raising up. I stop right in front of her and reach past to push the door gently shut, leaving my hand pressed against the door just above her shoulder. We're so close now. I should move away.

"I've missed you," I say instead. "As a friend, of course."

She moves her head back and forth with firm motion, breaking our gaze and shutting her eyes, as if to push an unwelcome thought out of her mind. I take that as a cue to give her more space, so I step back and let my hand drop to my side.

"I don't think we can be friends. I respect you wanting to get more involved. But here? With me? It's not a good idea."

Her words are a stab in my chest.

"I want to help. I want to make things right. Between us."

Britt's eyes fly open.

I wait for her to ask what I mean by that, but she doesn't. Thank fuck, because I don't know.

This isn't fair of me, and I know it.

"What I mean is, we're going to see each other all the time. You know, at school stuff. I think we can be friends."

She flinches. "Friends?"

"Acquaintances?" This time *I* flinch. "For Chelsea and Jackson's sake."

But it's more than that.

I have a lot to make up for, because I messed up so many times.

With Chelsea.

With Reese.

With Britt.

That feeling I had at the airport? Everything changed when I realized the meaning behind her words. I still don't understand the chaos that sprung up then and hasn't left me alone since. I think I just miss her friendship. But that feeling hasn't faded.

I can't get Britt out of my head.

But I'm not my mother, or my father. I didn't cheat on my wife, and I'm only here to be friends. I told Reese I had no feelings for Britt.

I take Britt's hands in mine. She lets me, her eyes shining, and the connection sends little tingles through my fingers up my arms.

"Please. And honestly? You need to find a hundred boxes of lights."

"Two weeks before Christmas." She bites her bottom lip and I resist the urge to reach out and run my thumb along that same spot where her tooth is making an indentation in her skin.

"Exactly. You may need the help, both physically and mentally. You'll need a strong constitution to visit that many stores."

"Alright," Britt says with a groan and half smile. "But I have to start in the morning. It's a Wednesday. Don't you have to work?"

I do, but I won't. Not if I have a chance to spend the day with Britt. Suddenly, it's the most important thing to me. Her hands are warm and I don't move. I don't want to scare her away.

"Nope. Took the day off."

A soft smile crosses her face, a breathtaking improvement from her pained expression five minutes ago.

"Heard you've been at CrossFit."

"Mmm-hmm. I started back a few weeks ago. You should too. Not sure how motivated I'll be to keep going without you."

She grins, then pulls her hands from mine, turning her palms up. "My lifting callouses are gone. I need to start working out again before I turn to mush."

"Never." The woman is far from mush, and I wish I could wrap my arms around her waist and pull her against me to prove my point. My eyes drift down over her body, and when I lift them back up, her cheeks are flushed.

She takes a step back, checking herself from what's going on between us.

Oh, fuck.

Friends. Friends. Friends.

I chant it in my head, hoping that'll help me keep myself in line. Friends don't head-to-toe check each other out. Neither do acquaintances. My face grows warm.

"Tomorrow." She swallows. "Pick me up at nine?"

"Absolutely."

Britt opens the door, letting the winter air rush back over me, like a bucket of ice water dumped over my head.

"Good night, Adrian."

With that, I leave, a slight spring to my step.

In the end, that turned out better than I'd imagined. It's the perfect plan, to be friends with Britt again, to make sure there's no awkwardness or hiding from each other at school events.

Nothing could possibly go wrong.

5

———————

BRITT

Oh, this is a bad idea.

I push the door shut behind Adrian and lean back against it, my hands splayed against the cold metal.

It makes sense that he'd want to get involved in school stuff now that he's a single dad. And smoothing things over between us is best for everyone. We will inevitably run into each other at school events for the next few years, and it'll be painful and awkward. I can't pull the dive-behind-a-group-of-parents move every time.

Besides, there's nothing between me and Adrian. Nothing to hide. I stopped it before it happened. That was the whole point in me stepping away. There was no physical contact. He was married to my best friend.

But in hindsight, there were earlier signs.

I'd sit next to him instead of across when we'd get a post-workout drink, and our thighs would touch as we chatted. He was always looking for excuses to touch me. An extra long hug, help putting my jacket on, lingering touches at the gym.

And the hug at the airport—the one where I pressed my body

against his—was not the norm. It was goodbye. I knew I'd messed up.

But that was my problem. It was one-sided, wasn't it? The fact that they got divorced anyway doesn't mean he reciprocated feelings.

What about just now, when it seemed he was ravaging me with his eyes? Did I imagine that?

I must've.

I close my lids. Dammit. That feeling is still there. Worse. And the warmth blossoming from my chest is a physical ache to have him touch me.

Doesn't matter. I can fight it off.

I come to life, wiping the coffee table and straightening couch cushions so the room is ready for the next morning. I place my mug upside down in the drying rack and freeze.

With Adrian being the bigger person and trying to make things normal or whatever between us, I should also finally summon the nerve to attempt peace with Reese. Surely, I can get her to listen to me. I'd apologize for whatever I did, for not being there for her divorce. Maybe even beg her to be friends again.

I miss her so much.

We used to write notes, like elementary school besties, and leave them on each other's windshields. Hers always made me cackle out loud. I could do something cheesy, like get her a friendship necklace. The little heart kind that's split in two and is popular amongst eight-year-old girls.

Then again, those necklaces remind me of a broken heart. Does she blame me for the divorce? She must. Otherwise, she'd have reached out. Or maybe she wants me to make the first move.

Captain materializes out of nowhere and presses his little gray body against my calves. He's always needy the nights Jackson stays with his father. That's when he's most likely to push a stack of papers off the table or casually swipe at the couch with his claws out. He's probably already hacked up a hairball in a corner. I squat down to stroke his silky fur just as my phone vibrates with an incoming text.

Adrian's name flashes on the screen. I suck my upper lip and click to expand the text.

ADRIAN

Hey. We'll hunt down every single remaining string of lights left in the state of New Jersey. And New York, if necessary. A trip to Pennsylvania might also be required

It's not normal how fast my heart beats, seeing his words in a text chain long since abandoned.

I should bail on tomorrow. Cut this thing off at the knees before it runs away on me.

Or, because that idea seems dreadful, I could work on squashing any of my remaining feelings for him. Yeah. Just run a giant dump truck over whatever lingering yearning remains in my sad little heart.

I'll go see Reese this weekend. It might take a hundred years, but I'll put in the time to make her understand how sorry I am. How much I miss her.

I'll start downloading dating apps and find my real true love.

Yeah, that'll work.

6

ADRIAN

Wednesday, December 13

Britt climbs into my SUV, bundled up in a puffy coat and thick scarf, phone in hand.

"Okay, I have a list. Let's start with the two big box stores across town." She keeps her eyes fixed on her screen.

I patiently wait for her to make eye contact with me.

Finally, she looks up. Her gaze falters when it meets mine. "Are we going?"

"Yeah, we're going."

"Sorry, that came out rude." Her cheeks pinken.

"When you get into an Uber, please look up and make sure you're in the right car." I smile at her, my eyes roaming her familiar face.

She's only sat in the front seat of my car a few times. The last time—not long before the airport event—she'd had a second drink after we worked out, so I drove her home. She'd sat next to me that night and laughed extra hard at my jokes. She'd let her hand linger on my forearm, and . . .

Oh, fuck.

How did I never notice?

But it's all ancient history now.

I lift my chin toward the cup holders. "I got us coffee."

The color deepens on her cheeks as she stares for another beat before looking down at the steaming beverages.

"Thank you." Britt picks up a cup and takes a sip, her eyes squinting with pleasure. "Perfect. We're going to need a lot of coffee to get through today."

"I'm looking forward to it. It's a challenge. We're Team Light Finders. Or, uh, Team Light It Up? You're better at the branding stuff. I'm just a numbers guy."

She rolls her head to me and blinks a hundred times, one for each box of lights we need to locate. "We're just looking for lights. Okay?" But there's a twinkle in her eye.

"All business. Got it." I nod.

"Let's go then." She gestures to the road.

We're quiet until we pull up to the first store five minutes later.

"How's Jackson?" I follow her through the parking lot, entering the store side by side through sliding doors.

"He's great." But she crinkles the sides of her face for a brief second, and I'm not sure I believe her. "Oh, this way." Britt directs us to the seasonal displays. "My ex and I are doing well co-parenting. It feels like we finally figured it all out. It only took four years."

I grunt. How long will it be before Reese and I are like that? It doesn't help that at fourteen, Chelsea is a fully functional mini-adult, so Reese and I don't have to exchange a ton of information.

"I'm happy for you."

"Wait, are they really playing Metallica?" Britt steals a glance at me. "That's about as un-Christmasy as you can get."

"Has Metallica not released a holiday album? Surely they've done a remake of *Joy to the World*."

"Ha," Britt says, a smile cracking her face as she pivots down an aisle. Then screeches to a halt in front of a whole lot of nothing. "Oh, no."

"Well, this isn't good." I survey the empty shelves.

A few sad extension cords lay abandoned where the lights should be. Not a single box. A small, fuzzy tumbleweed of dust drifts across the shelf. Another heavy metal song roars through the loudspeakers.

Also not Christmas music.

"What are we going to do?" Britt turns to me, face etched with the start of panic.

"We're going to go to the next store, that's what we'll do." I gently pull her arm and direct her away from the vacant shelves.

"But what if there are no lights? And why was that music so angry?"

"We have a billion stores we can check out. Either way, the kids will have a blast at the dance. You know that, right? You are not responsible for ensuring that each individual kid has fun."

She groans. "It feels like I am."

"Come on." We climb into my car and set the navigation for store number two.

Ten minutes later, we're only slightly more successful.

"Three boxes?" Britt turns to me, her face at the second stage of panic as she clutches the lights to her chest like they're the last three cans of black beans in the apocalypse.

I shrug. "We can probably light up one whole doorway."

"You're not funny." A shadow of a grin crosses her face.

"But listen." I gesture above us, where classic holiday tune *White Christmas* sounds through the store's loudspeakers. "At least the music is better. Although who doesn't love a little eighties hair band?"

"I do not. I'm going to go pay for these."

"Let me see your store list." I accept her phone and follow Britt to the self-checkout. "Oh, I have a good feeling about the next one." I wiggle the phone. "It's a little farther out. But it's bigger."

And according to the map, there's a coffee shop right around the corner.

"You think?" She bags the three boxes of lights.

I need to make this right for her. A surge of energy flows through me. We are going to find enough damn lights if it kills me.

"I do. Let's go!" I grab her hand and pull her toward the door. We burst out of the sliding doors.

She screeches to a halt on the sidewalk and gasps. "It's starting to snow!"

A few fat white flakes drift down from the sky.

"See? The holiday spirit is with us." I watch Britt close her eyes and turn her face up to the light snow.

She smiles, eyes still shut.

"Ten. That's pretty good!" Britt's pulling the boxes into her arms—we didn't get a cart so as to not jinx the operation—and counting to herself.

"Ten's amazing! Enough for, like, three doorways, and maybe the DJ table." I tilt my head. "Remind me, how many are we looking for?"

She groans. "One hundred. But you knew that."

A chuckle bubbles up in my chest and she gives me a narrow-eyed look.

"What?"

"A hundred is just . . . a lot," I say. "At the rate of zero, three, or ten a store, we have a long way to go."

She giggles, a pained moan underneath it.

"The next one, we're going to hit the jackpot," I insist. "I can feel it."

Her giggles evolve into laughter, and I can't help but join her. Two of the boxes fall out of her arms and I face her after picking them up. Tears of laughter roll down her cheeks.

This is perfect. This is exactly how I want to spend my day. My days. With Britt. Laughing.

Woah. Hold up.

I check my thoughts and grab boxes from Britt's arms, following her to the front of the store, the occasional chuckle still sounding from her.

Maybe we can do more than smooth things over.

Maybe we can be friends.

Maybe we can be more?

But no. She doesn't want that. And I don't either. I want to be logical, safe, and steady. For Chelsea. Not fall in love with my ex-wife's ex-best friend.

What?

Who is talking love, anyway? Not me. And not Britt. She needed space, and then I abandoned her.

The snow's falling harder now, and when we exit the store, Britt spins in circles and laughs, twirling in the falling flakes. My heart squeezes, and when she inevitably gets dizzy, I step forward and let her lean against me.

"It's so beautiful, don't you think?"

"Sure is." She's watching the snow, but I'm watching her.

The backseat is filling up with bags of lights and Britt's looking hopeful, but inside, I'm in turmoil, right back where I was six months ago, when I was confused about what was going on, both in my marriage and between me and Britt.

Instead of driving to the next store, I turn into the coffee shop I'd seen on the map.

"Where are we going?"

"We need fuel. Quick caffeine break? And a muffin or a cake pop to celebrate?"

"I'm not sure we deserve it yet, with only thirteen boxes." She gestures to the backseat.

"How about we get the most ridiculous holiday drink we can find? Maybe that'll bring us luck." I maneuver my SUV into a spot and turn the car off. "Look how cozy it is in there."

Through falling snow, the glass windows of the coffee shop

display holiday decorations. A giant Christmas tree towers in one corner, rainbow lights twinkling. A bookcase adorned with white, silver, and shades of blue lights show off a small menorah.

Britt's eyes shine. "Fine. It does look lovely in there."

I offer her my arm on the snow-covered sidewalk, and she slips her hand through my elbow. Inside, the store is as atmospheric as it looked from the parking lot, and even as a line builds up behind us, the world's happiest baristas take our order for peppermint mochas with extra whipped cream and chocolate shavings on top, adorned with a candy cane and a hand-drawn snowflake instead of a dot above the letter *I* in our names.

"This is an absolutely ridiculous drink." We settle onto a couch, and even though I'm careful to leave a slight space between us, the worn cushions cave in so we end up with our thighs touching lightly.

"You promised me the *most* ridiculous holiday beverage." Britt's tongue darts out and wipes a blob of whipped cream off her top lip.

"Is it everything you dreamed of?" I resist the urge to reach out and swipe the bit she missed. She grins and nods, sucking the candy cane in between her lips, having no idea what she's doing to me. Jesus. I look away. A middle-aged couple walks in the door, holding hands and snuggling into each other.

"How are things with you and Reese?"

I take a sharp breath, not intending for it to be so audible.

"Could be worse. Could be better. We're not quite the co-parenting stars that you and your ex are."

"You'll get there," she says.

"I feel like a bad person." The words spill out of my mouth, but they ring true. They're the ones I think all the time but never verbalize.

"No, Adrian . . ."

"Wait, let me finish. Not because of you." I turn my body toward hers, and she does the same. We're so close. "You know how my parents were. I'm sure your brother told you stories. They were always fighting, making up, then cheating again. It was horrible. And after they got divorced, it was worse. They didn't talk to each other, but just communicated through me and my brother. To this day, they haven't spoken since their divorce—including at my wedding."

"I'm so sorry." Britt's now fully facing me.

"Don't be. I just want Reese and I to have the best chance at co-parenting. And I haven't done a good job so far. She won't really talk to me outside of text messages."

"It's all my fault. I tried to remove myself from the situation, but I'd already screwed things up." Britt's face crumples and she bites her lower lip. "I'm just sorry, A."

Her old nickname for me slips out of her mouth so easily, and it's natural for me to reach for her hand. She takes it without hesitation, linking our fingers together.

"Don't be sorry." I want to say more, but we're on dangerous ground here. Holding hands, spending the day together, dancing around what happened, talking about it, but also not really at all.

How do I feel about her? I want to kiss her—I know that. I want to pull her to me and peel that heavy jacket off.

She rubs her thumb against the inside of my wrist and there's a stirring in my groin. This is lust. Not love. Maybe she was confused as well. She thought she was developing real feelings for me, but they weren't.

The thing is, this doesn't *feel* like just lust.

She pulls her hand away. "Let's get going. We have eighty-six more boxes to find."

I laugh. "Eighty-seven. Doable, I'd think." We toss our empty drinks—a serious sugar high is coming—and climb back into the car. "My phone says the next store is twenty minutes away." I start the navigation.

"This better be the one."

"It will be. I promised you we'd hit the jackpot, remember?"

"I remember." A smile is in her voice, and I match it on my face.

~

WE WALK into the next store, hands no longer linked, but arms brushing against each other. Britt leads us directly to the aisle where the lights would be.

"Holy shit!" she screeches. An employee, wearing a Santa hat and struggling to fit boxes of lights from his cart onto the shelves, jumps back at her yelp.

"Sorry," I say to him. But I can't keep my eyes off of Britt as she surveys what we've found.

There are so many boxes of lights, they fill the shelves from top to bottom. She turns to me, mouth hanging open, eyes wide, hands in the air, pure joy on her face.

"Think this will be enough?" I ask.

The employee skitters away, terrified.

"Yes!" Britt jumps up and throws her arms around my neck in a celebratory hug, then stills and keeps her body against mine, head nuzzled in my chest. Warmth explodes in my body. Our hearts are beating in rhythm, our open jackets keeping only two layers of fabric between us.

Britt is in my arms.

I place my hands around her waist on the outside of her jacket.

"Congrats," I whisper in her ear.

She turns her face up to me and our lips are mere inches away. I want nothing more than to bring our mouths together, to see if I can remember how it feels to kiss Britt, to test how soft her lips are, to see if I can taste the coffee we just drank.

She slides her arms down from my neck and leans back. I lean forward and kiss her forehead, pausing for a beat with my lips on her skin before releasing her from my embrace. She steps back and crosses her arms on her chest.

Did that cross a boundary? Probably. But I'm not sure I care anymore.

"Thank you for your help today." Her voice is almost a whisper.

"I'm not done helping. Let's count these puppies and make sure we don't need anything else. When do we decorate?"

Her face contorts, going through several emotions, but landing on one that I can't quite identify.

It's a good one. That much I know.

"Friday afternoon?"

"Of course." I'd do anything for her. I'll take off the rest of the week if it means spending time with her again.

"We need a cart."

"Let me get it. You count the goods." I stride down the aisle to the front of the store with a bounce in my step. My heart is beating wildly and I feel Britt in every cell of my body.

A minute later, I race back to the aisle with a cart, pausing for a second to watch her touch the boxes, one by one. Her forehead crinkles, eyes laser focused. She turns and catches me watching her.

It doesn't faze her. A giant smile crosses her face. "Eighty-seven boxes. This is it. We're done!"

I grin at her, starting to understand how deep my feelings for this woman run. Something inside me shifts.

Ah, fuck.

We're friends, and I'm attracted to her. That's where it has to stop.

Even though we have all the boxes we need, I know we're not done.

And I have a feeling we never will be.

7

BRITT

Friday, December 15

"Should we have picked up more lights?" I press my palms on either side of my face. Adrian and I stand at the entrance to the high school gym and survey our work.

Adrian laughs, an easy sound that envelops me like a warm blanket. I glance at him and smile.

"The taxpayers will be happy you didn't spend more on decorations for this dance." There's a twinkle in his eyes when he meets my gaze.

Adrian's wearing a thin t-shirt that hugs his CrossFit muscles and makes my insides turn to goo. No way he had planned to take two days off this week. I know that. He took them off to help me, not only spending most of the day hunting for lights on Wednesday but showing up four hours ago to prep the gym and string those lights around the large room.

Lights outline the windows and doors, then go up and over the pushed-in bleachers. There was even enough to adorn the activity tables: the photo booth with funny masks and a station with buckets of soft white balls for fake snowball fights. But with the afternoon sun streaming in the windows, it's hard to tell just how magical the lights will look tonight.

The past few days have been the most fun I've had in months.

Even Jackson noticed. When he got home from school on Wednesday afternoon, he was like, *What's up with you, Mom? Why are you smiling?* And in return, I smiled even broader.

Me being happy makes Jackson happy? Who knew?

For the first time in forever, I feel like I'm doing something right for my son. And for myself.

Adrian grins and throws his arm around my shoulder as if it's the most natural thing in the world.

"Imagine it, Britt." He sweeps a hand over the expanse of the gym. "In just a few hours, hundreds of horny, sweaty teens and preteens will converge in this very spot."

I giggle and reach up to touch the hand hanging off my shoulder, feeling like a teenager myself. We stare at each other, and my laughter fades into background music.

I wonder if this could be okay, the way I'm feeling right now.

But nothing's changed—not really—since Adrian first walked into the Idea Garage a few days ago. No matter my good intentions, I still messed up my friendship with Reese, whatever I had with Adrian, and their marriage. I don't deserve this feeling that's growing inside me—a tiny wisp of a plant that was shriveled up and mostly dead in the dark, cold shade of winter, but that is starting to perk up now that it feels a small ray of sunlight.

"Adrian," I whisper. "I . . ."

"Britt!" A voice rings out across the gym and I reluctantly turn to see the mom trio of Jill, Sara, and Liz waving at me.

"Oh, god. You better go deal with the moms." Adrian drops his arm from my shoulder. "But I'm going to avoid them. Is it better if they ignore you, or acknowledge you? I can't figure it out."

I turn to him, my mouth still open and ready to say something.

What was I going to say? I'm not sure, but I should probably thank the moms for interrupting.

"Yeah." I take a step away. "Smart. I'd avoid contact, to be honest." We hold our gaze for another second, then I shake my head to clear it. "I'll check in with them, then I'm going to head out so I can get dressed and be back before the kids arrive. See you later?"

Adrian runs his hand through his hair, letting a thick piece fall on his forehead. He was a flirt as a teenager. I watched him and my brother from a distance. Adrian didn't give me a second glance until that one kiss at the party after high school graduation.

Then, nothing.

He's definitely glancing at me now.

"I wouldn't miss it. Save me a dance?"

I bite my lip and nod before spinning around and heading across the gym.

A FEW HOURS LATER, I'm back and bouncing from one station to the next, making sure everything is absolutely perfect.

It is. I'm so damn excited to see all the kids walk in. It feels like it's *my* winter dance, too.

And Adrian was right. It was impossible to tell the effect of the strings of lights this afternoon, but I'm glad I listened to him and the moms, who insisted that we needed so many of them. It is perfect. I have no regrets about the cost. What taxpayers? What PTO? I'd fund this all myself if I had to. Jackson was bouncing with excitement when I dropped him off at his friend's house a few hours ago. He and his buddy want to make an entrance tonight together. I smile and shake my head. What a funny kid.

I stop by the music booth, where corporate mom Grace is chatting with the DJ. She wiggles a few fingers at me and goes back to talking to him. She has a clipboard, so she must know what she's doing.

The dance starts in just ten minutes, and kids are already lining up to get in. Jackson will sleep at his friend's house tonight, which means he doesn't have to hang around the gym while I clean up. I can't wait for him to see this place. A goofy smile grows on my face and warmth radiates from the center of my chest. Tonight, I want to forget about how I messed up in the past year. The night is about Jackson and all the kids having an amazing time at their dance. This is going to be a good night for him. For everyone. I just know it.

I smooth my dress down, hoping I didn't overdo it with my tall, skinny heels and strapless, sparkly black dress, the one I'd bought for a night out in New York City a few years ago. What was the name of the guy I went with? Brad? Robert? Oh, I think it was Brendan. Maybe. Who knows? Who cares? He didn't mean anything to me.

Not like Adrian does.

My stomach squeezes as I imagine Adrian throwing his arm over my shoulder now, my bare skin under his palm, leaning in to whisper something in my ear.

"Get it under control, Britt." Music echoes from the huge speakers, drowning out the sound of me pep talking myself. Everything is going to be perfect tonight. I can't get lost in my own head. That's how I got myself into this mess.

The first students burst into the gym, a group of kids from Jackson's grade. Two girls clutching each other's arms stare wide-eyed at the lights, giggling and doing little excited jumps, looking super trendy with their short dresses paired with bright white sneakers.

Jackson appears in the third group and I wave eagerly. He lifts a hand to say hello, not yet ashamed of acknowledging his mom in front of friends. They smile and look around with wonder.

Jackson mouths the word *wow* to the other boy. Happy fireworks burst inside of me.

All the work was worth it.

I pull my hair over my shoulder, not used to it being down and curled. I tried way too hard tonight. No one cares what I look like. Adrian will barely notice my dress or my heels or the effort I put into my hair. My phone vibrates and I grab it out of the clutch purse hanging off my wrist. I sigh. It's just a text about trash delivery around the holidays being delayed.

While I'm there, I scroll to my text chain with Adrian, which was quiet for so long but now filled with messages from the last few days. Messages about nothing, really, just a picture of his Christmas tree at his new place, him asking what I got the app incubator team, an image of Captain shredding toilet paper, him sending some stupid meme that made me laugh . . .

I slip my phone back into my bag. I could use a drink. Something to cool me down. Maybe a cold shower instead.

Chelsea walks in with two of her friends. She's two years older than Jackson, but I know her group almost as well as his from Reese's stories. She scans the room but quickly turns away from where I'm standing. Maybe she doesn't see me, but most likely she does and is continuing to blow me off. I don't blame her. She hasn't acknowledged me since I announced my break from their family. I curl my hands in and out of fists, regretting how things went down, wishing I could do it all over again. The right way.

But was there a right way? I thought that's what I was doing.

I ended up alone, anyway.

Chelsea and her friends join another group of giggling girls standing at the edge of the dance floor.

"You look beautiful, Britt."

I snap my head to Adrian, standing next to me dressed in a full tuxedo, one hand in his pocket, looking like some kind of suburban dad version of James Bond.

"Hi," I squeak and soak in his freshly shaven jaw, lightly styled hair, and wide, dark eyes trained on me.

His eyes drift down my neck, bare shoulders, over the curve of my breasts, and down to my exposed legs. A shiver runs up my spine as he raises his gaze back to my face. Adrian takes a step toward me and I imagine him pulling me in close against his body, kissing my neck.

"It looks gorgeous in here. You did a spectacular job."

I nod, still mute, thinking about him calling me beautiful. He lifts his hands and places one on each of my upper arms, slowly sliding them down until they reach my elbows.

"Hey. You okay?" His brow furrows and he leans toward me, so close.

"Of course." The tingles from his touch break my freeze. "Sorry, I was just . . . overwhelmed for a second. A tux, huh?"

He grins and drops his hands to do his James Bond pose again. "I needed to show these kids how you get dressed up for a lady."

"Which lady would that be?" I look over my shoulder as if there's some formally dressed woman lingering behind me.

Adrian chuckles. "Where's the bar? Surely there's a chaperone-only bar?"

"Um. High school and middle school dance? No bar. But I wish there were."

"See, this is why I never volunteer."

The DJ's voice booms from the speakers, announcing the first slow song of the night. Romantic guitar strums fill the gym.

"How about that dance?"

Butterflies explode in every part of my body as Adrian holds his hand out to me. How could I say no? Should I? Not a chance. I put my hand in his. He turns to the middle of the gym, then hesitates, scanning the room.

"Hey." I gently tug his hand, and when he shifts his gaze to me, I nod my head toward the curtained supply area behind us, which

I know is piled with cases of water, snacks, storage bins, and other dance items.

He cringes, but relief floods his face as well. "It's better the kids don't see us, okay?"

"I agree. Now come on."

I lead Adrian around the curtain, and as soon as we're behind it, he pulls me into his arms, sliding one hand around my waist, grasping my other hand with his and holding it up by our shoulders. We keep eye contact and I'm sure he can feel the blood rushing through my body like molten lava in a volcano. We remain a few inches apart, and I have to hold back from pressing my full body against his. God, I want to feel him against me.

"Just so you know, I have no problem with us dancing together. Hanging out together. I just wouldn't want the kids to see us and speculate, you know?"

I breathe out. "Not that there's anything to speculate on, right? I feel like there's been enough speculation in this area to last us a lifetime."

He blinks about a billion times and moves his hand gently on the small of my back, sending sparks to my core. I close my eyes for a beat. I wish away the guilt that's attempting to suffocate me.

"Britt. Look at me."

I drag open my eyes, drowning in the intensity that I find in his.

"I'm looking."

"You know you're a good person, right? The best person."

"No." I shake my head, and we're back to having this conversation. I don't think we're capable of small talk. "A good person doesn't do what I did."

I still can't talk about it directly.

"Listen to me. I am telling you, you're the most authentic human I have ever met. You should not feel bad about what happened. Never feel bad. You didn't do anything wrong. All you did was remove yourself from the situation, like any good person would do. Reese and I were going to split up. You just made us see it sooner rather than later."

The breath disappears from my lungs. "That doesn't exactly sound like something a good person would do." But hearing him say it is everything.

He lets out a low chuckle. "Being honest with yourself and others around you? You tried to protect us by doing the right thing. Most people would not have done that."

I furrow my brow and press my lips together. "I messed it all up, Adrian."

He presses his palm against my lower back and moves his other hand to my waist, flush against him. Adrian leans forward to speak directly into my ear. "No, you didn't. You did exactly what I needed you to do. Thank you. Reese and I are better off apart. It's been that way for a long time. You saved me. I just didn't know it at the time."

I don't know how to respond. But my body is doing it for me, melting into his, and we've certainly crossed the line to inappropriate at a school function. Thank god for the curtain. I wrap my arms tighter around his neck. He breathes in and out heavily.

"What're you saying?" My voice is airy, wispy.

"I don't know."

Emotions overwhelm me. His lips are still an inch from my ear, so close I can feel his hot breath. His hand holds my hips pressed against him and the hard length against my stomach tells me that he wants me, at least right now.

I love this man.

Oh, no.

In his arms, I can finally admit to myself that I am madly in love with Adrian Whitlock.

Maybe it was too late to stop even six months ago.

I'd kept the feelings in a locked box from the second I left the airport, and now they've burst out and grown exponentially. I'd hoped we could make things less awkward between us, so we could see each other at functions—like this one—without it being terribly painful. But now all I want to do is peel his tux off one piece at a time and ravage him.

I love him, but what does he feel for me? What does this mean for us? Can I let myself have this man? This life? What about Reese?

Maybe I don't have to move on from him. Maybe I can have him. Maybe I'm not a pile of trash for doing what I did.

Maybe I was following my heart, and the universe will reward me for that.

We sway back and forth, and I hope the song will last forever.

8

ADRIAN

The lights are on and the remaining kids are waiting out front for their rides. It's just the vendors packing up their equipment and late volunteers cleaning up the mess left behind by the students.

I can't keep my eyes off Britt taking down a strand of lights five feet from me. She's insisting that she and I dismantle and pack all the lights ourselves, because heaven forbid another volunteer puts our hard-won decor away incorrectly. Slipping off her heels, she climbs a short ladder and reaches above a doorframe to unhook the last light strand. I should stop her and do it myself, but instead, I steady the ladder, watching her stretch her body up high, the top hem of her dress moving down a few inches and revealing more of her back.

I'm frozen until she turns to me and smiles.

"Can you let me climb the ladder next time?" I throw my hands up when she's back on the gym floor.

"It's hardly a ladder. More like a step stool." But she grins and rolls the strand into a neat pile in one of the new plastic bins that is just about full. "And we're all done, I think."

When I look at her, I feel all the things I've been fighting against my entire life. Emotions so intense they overwhelm me. I'd do anything to pull her behind that curtain again.

For once, I don't feel bad about wanting to give in to those emotions. I don't feel like I'm making the mistakes my parents did, because this feels right and good. Not destructive nor forbidden. I can't define what I feel. Just lust? Really intense lust? No. It's more than that. Affection? Friendship, along with the lust?

I'd wanted to dance with her every time a slow song came on, but she was always running around making sure everything was going smoothly.

Maybe she was avoiding me and whatever is happening between us.

"Want to help me find this mysterious storage room?" She bends down and picks up a box of lights.

"Yes, I do, but give me that before you lose your whole dress carrying it across the gym."

Britt laughs and I close the gap between us and slide my arms along the bottom of the bin, our hands meeting at the center of the container. We stop, our fingers touching, both of us smiling. I see a flush creeping up her neck and feel a stirring in my dick as I imagine the bin tugging her dress further down.

Across the gym by the entrance, a loud crash draws my attention. Two parents and the caterer are cleaning a mess of metal trays and lids.

And Chelsea stands in the middle of the doorway, watching us with arms crossed.

Oh no. I would wave, but my hands are full, so instead I press my lips together in an attempt at a smile.

We aren't doing anything wrong, but it's clear from my daughter's stiff back and narrowed eyes that she's not impressed. Fuck. She spins and disappears before I can react.

Britt follows my glance but doesn't see Chelsea.

"Oh, just trays? They've got it covered. Let's get this bin put away."

"I'll follow you." I heft up the heavy container of lights, wishing I'd taken off my tux jacket and loosened the bowtie first. I'll need to talk to Chelsea. I'll need to figure out how to explain to her what's going on with Britt. But how will I do that when even I don't know? I shake my head, trying to clear it of worry about Chelsea. For now.

"I'm not one hundred percent certain where this closet is." Britt leads me down the school hallway lined with lockers and through a set of double doors. "The PTO moms gave me directions."

I follow her through a gate with a No Students Allowed sign and down a flight of steps to the dimly lit lower level.

"Are you sure you're not taking me somewhere to murder me?" I hope she's planning on making out with me down here instead, like a couple of high school kids sneaking into a forbidden area.

She glances back over her shoulder and smiles. I'm so glad I get to have that smile directed at me again. It feels as if the clouds have parted in our gray skies after too long.

"I know. It's a bit isolated. Oh, I think this is it." Britt stops in front of a closet door and pulls it open. The air inside feels moist, and it's dark and dingy.

"Gross." I drop the bin at my feet.

"Well, shit," she says. "Someone was supposed to clean this all up." The floor of the closet has puddles of water on it. Britt sniffs the air and sticks her hands on her hips, scrunching her nose. "Oh no."

"It smells like rotten mice carcasses."

"Ew. And I was supposed to call maintenance. Damn! And now the school's closed for the holidays, so it won't get done until January."

"Hey, not a big deal. Can we leave them in the gym over the holiday break?"

Right now, I couldn't care less about the bins. I'm watching Britt. She pulls her hair over her shoulder and bites her lower lip, staring into the closet.

She lets out a nondescript sound and shakes her head. "They're pretty strict about stuff like that. Fire codes or something. But I can take them to my house for a few weeks. I have the space."

Britt turns to me and freezes at the look on my face. I can only imagine what she sees there, but if it matches the tornado of desire that I feel inside, no wonder her eyes grow wide.

As we stare at one another, the longest moment passes. Her eyes flit down to my mouth and she licks her lips.

Now's the time. I have to take my chance with her.

I step forward and reach out to touch her hair before sliding my fingers along her neck, around the back of her head. Her eyes close and she breathes deeply, as if she can't catch her breath.

"Britt."

"Mmm."

"Open your eyes." I need her to look at me. Know how fucking incredible she is.

Her eyes flutter open and she comes to life, closing the remaining inches between our bodies, pulling me in by my waist so our pelvises press together. I breathe in sharply.

"I need you to kiss me right now, Adrian. Don't make me beg."

Without hesitation, I kiss her lips. Nothing has ever felt as right as this moment. The room spins lazily with our lips pressed together, as if I'm tipsy, and I know with certainty that I could stand here in this basement for the rest of my life kissing this woman.

She leans into my mouth and flicks her tongue onto mine, driving me wild and causing my cock to immediately harden. She pulls away and stares at me with hooded eyes and a sexy, lazy smile on her lips.

"Fuck, Britt," I say. I've lost any cool I ever had. How could I have ever questioned my feelings for her? I wish I could go back to that night in the airport and kiss her. Just like this. I know why I didn't. If we had done it that way, I would have lost her. I know Britt. She didn't want anything to happen. Kissing her back then would have been the wrong way on so many levels.

"I've thought about kissing you more than I'd like to admit," she murmurs. Her lips are extra red. But when I move in to kiss her again, she leans away. I take a few beats to attempt to calm down with deep breaths, but it's hopeless.

"Adrian," she says like it's a prayer.

And maybe it is. Maybe she's asking for help, for guidance. Maybe she's still trying to resist this thing between us.

I don't move my hand from where it's buried in her hair. "These past few days, Britt, they've been so incredible, and I've . . ."

"Britt?" A voice calls from just up the stairs and Britt steps back abruptly, breaking our physical contact.

"Yeah?" she squeaks. "We, uh, can't use the closet. It's too gross."

Liz appears at the bottom of the stairs, tilting her head and taking in the scene with raised eyebrows.

"You don't want the other bins brought down here?" A small, curious smile crosses her face.

Britt shakes her head and won't look at me. "No. We're coming up with this one now."

"Okay." Liz takes one last look back and forth between us and heads up the stairs.

"That was close." A chuckle escapes my mouth when we're alone.

Britt turns to me, her cheeks red, lips redder, half-smiling.

"Let's go upstairs."

I follow her back through the basement with the bin positioned in front of me like a shield.

Somehow, Britt's got me wrapped right around her little finger.

And god help me, I'll follow her anywhere.

9

————

BRITT

"Can you help me get the bins to my house?"

"Huh?" Though we're back in the gym, Adrian still looks dazed from our kiss in the basement. Who knows what could have happened if Liz hadn't interrupted us? What would he have said? What would *I* have said?

Dingy basement or not, I would've agreed to anything he asked of me.

I don't know what he feels, but I'm not planning on telling him I'm madly in love with him. I know he wants me, physically at least. I could feel it when we danced behind the curtain. When we kissed in the basement.

"Can you help me? Load them into my car?" I nod at the stack of bins filled with lights and decorations. "And into my house?"

Oh god. What am I doing? But I know. I know exactly what I'm doing right now.

I know what I want.

"Your house?" His eyes grow wide. Wider.

"Yes." I bite my lip and grin at him, head tilted. Am I being charming and seductive? That's the goal. "Get in your car and follow me home, then help me unload the lights. Into my house."

My house, where we'll be alone. My house, that has my bed in it.

He blinks, examining my face, trying to figure out if this is something more than it seems to be.

As usual, I realize this is the wrong way to do things. There will be no going back after spending the night with Adrian, but I'll worry about that tomorrow. For now, there's some kind of magic happening between us. Sparks and spells and a huge freaking bonfire.

I can't let this chance slip by.

Now I know my separation from Adrian and Reese didn't work. Without them—without *him*—my feelings only grew, like invasive weeds in an untended garden.

Or maybe it's more beautiful than simple weeds.

Maybe it's more like beautiful wildflowers.

I direct him to my car with the five giant bins, which don't fit in my mid-sized trunk, so he sticks them in the back of his SUV.

Do I have to take the bins home? Probably not. I made up the part about the school being really strict about leaving stuff in the gym.

Could they have sat there until something else was arranged?

Yup, they sure could've.

But this way, I have an excuse to take Adrian home, along with the bins. I'm sick of waiting. I'm sick of feeling bad about myself.

One night together.

That's all this will be. That's all we can have.

I PRESS the garage door opener, but as usual, the battery is cranky so it doesn't work. Adrian jumps out of his car and strides up, tapping my code into the keypad. This man knows my garage code, for fuck's sake. I slip out of the car.

"You should really change that once in a while." He grins.

I shrug, my face flushing. He's always been able to come and go. And I really like that idea.

Adrian unloads the bins into my one-car garage, then wordlessly follows me through the door to the main part of my house. By the time I stop in the middle of the kitchen, my chest is thumping and I'm questioning whether he wants to be here or if he'll even want to kiss me again.

But I no longer wonder if I'm doing the right thing. I know the answer to that.

"Want a drink?" I fiddle with the zipper on my coat. A soft light spills in from the lit Christmas tree in my family room, and holiday music from one of my smart devices echos softly throughout the house.

He nods and slips off his own jacket while I pull a bottle of red wine from the small wine rack on my kitchen counter. As I open the bottle, he grabs stemmed glasses from the correct cabinet on the first try.

In silence, I pour the wine, and we both drink, our eyes locked. I gnaw on my bottom lip and slip my jacket off, hanging it on the counter stool, aware of all my bare skin.

Adrian's eyes roam over my body. Am I brave enough to do this? To seduce Adrian?

"You look beautiful tonight." He repeats his earlier compliment, a slight wobble in his voice.

I swallow and slide my glass onto the counter, stepping toward him until I'm a foot away. His pupils expand when I take the glass out of his hands and push it onto the counter.

It's now or never.

"You said that already." My voice is a whisper.

I reach behind me to grab the zipper on my dress, then tug it down. His eyes bulge, mouth dropping open with the crackle of the zipper. Feeling bolder than I ever have, I push the dress down to uncover my bare breasts, then wiggle it over my hips and onto the floor in a heap.

I'm standing in front of him wearing nothing but four-inch heels and white lace underwear already soaked with desire for him.

His eyes roam my body, landing on my breasts, roving over the curve of my hips and the length of my legs.

Adrian moans and steps forward. "You're the most beautiful woman I've ever seen." He ravishes my body with his stare.

I breathe in and out, my chest rising and falling. He wants to be with me. Physically, of course. I'll take it. There's a throbbing ache in my nipples and between my legs. I can't believe this is happening. After all the yearning, all the angst, and the unrequited feelings, here we are.

Even if it's just for tonight.

"Adrian," I whisper and reach out to him, placing my hands on his chest. If he doesn't touch me soon, I'm going to explode.

"I . . ." He stops himself from saying more and instead lowers his face to mine, covering my mouth with his, sliding his hands around my waist and down over my ass. His touch is like fire—it's as if he's leaving behind burn marks on my skin.

I groan, acutely aware that I'm almost naked and he's fully dressed, my hard nipples rubbing against his tuxedo shirt. It's hot as hell, but I'm desperate to feel his skin against mine, so I unbutton his shirt, starting from the top.

A squeak escapes my throat as his mouth roams to my neck and over my right breast, his tongue flicking my nipple. I lose hold of the button. Adrian pauses and looks up at me, pulling back.

"Britt," he growls.

My voice is gone, but I manage to whisper, "Yes?"

He straightens and pulls my body against his, looking deep into my eyes.

"Do you want this? *Really* want this?"

Beneath layers of escalating desire, there's something else inside me. Fear. Desperation. This is the man I love, about to take all of me. Once we cross that line, there will be no going back. Not for me, anyway. There will be no easy congeniality at school events or pretending we're just friends. No denying I'm in love with him.

I wish I wasn't too chicken to ask how he feels.

"I really want this, A." My voice returns and with it, my ability to unbutton. My fingers go back to work on the buttons and soon he's free enough that I can pull his shirt out from his pants, exposing his hard, muscled abs, spiraling down to tuxedo pants, which are tented with his hard cock. "I've never wanted anything more."

"Thank fuck, because I'm not sure I could let you go right now. I would, of course, if you told me to stop."

"Don't stop," I say, mesmerized by the growing need in his voice.

He takes one of my hands and lowers it to his groin, moaning as I grasp the length of him through his pants. "Fuck." He groans.

I'm gonna let this go all the way. It already has, for me.

Adrian slides a hand down my stomach and slips a finger in between my legs, stroking back and forth. A moan comes out, and it doesn't even sound like me. Carnal desire takes over. I'll save freaking out for later. Adrian and I are together, touching each other, the heat and friction between us almost unbearable. It's my ultimate fantasy.

"I've been thinking about this." Adrian pushes his hand further into my underwear, pulsing two fingers inside of me. "So much more than is appropriate. I thought about how you'd feel on the inside."

"And how do I feel?" I rasp into his ear, shocked I can get a word out, moving my hips against his fingers.

"Fucking wet and amazing."

I groan and arch my back as his hand moves between my legs.

A shattering of glass on the counter startles both of us and we freeze.

Captain sits next to a broken wine glass spread across the

counter. Watching us with his grumpy face. Judging. Giggles spill out of my mouth as my cat stares at us.

"Should we clean that up?" Adrian's voice is filled with dread.

"I have to." With great regret, I push Adrian's hand away. "I'll be quick. Get out of here, Captain." I wave my hand and the cat jumps off the counter and stalks away, his objective of interrupting us achieved.

Adrian's breathing heavy and I turn my back to him, picking up a few of the big pieces of glass and tossing them in the trash. When I grab paper towels, Adrian presses up against me from behind, gently running his hands up my sides, rubbing his groin against my ass.

"Hurry, baby." He buries his head in my neck and reaches around for one of my breasts, trapping me in a heated embrace against the counter. "You look so hot in those heels."

"You're not making this easy," I pant, unable to stop myself from grinding back against him. The counter is clean enough, and I reach down and tug my underwear down so my bare ass is pressed up against his cock, still covered with tuxedo pants. His free hand slips back between my legs and he fingers me, pulling me tighter against him.

I move against him, desperate for more. But I want to be in control. Tonight, I *am* in control. I spin around and step out of my underwear as I meet his eyes, which are hooded, pupils as big as his irises. I fumble with the button on his pants and push him back toward the kitchen table, my heels clicking on the hardwood floor.

"Sit," I whisper, just as I get the button undone and manage to slip his pants over his hips, freeing his erection, leaving only a thin fabric between us. I run my hand in between the elastic of his boxers and his abdomen, savoring the rippling of his muscles at my touch before tugging them down. His cock springs up against my hand.

Adrian flips a chair around, collapsing into it and looking up at me. I climb on top of him, lowering my naked body onto his. He groans when I make contact with him, moving my hips, skin against skin. He breathes heavily against my neck.

"I want you inside me, A. Please tell me you have protection?" Because I do not. I'm a single mom who doesn't date.

He leans back and looks into my eyes. "Fuck, Britt, I don't."

"I haven't been with someone in years," I say. "And I'm on the pill."

"I haven't been with anyone since . . ."

I cover his lips with mine, not wanting to hear the end of the sentence. "Then I want you inside me as you are."

Adrian moans and thrusts his tongue in my mouth. My need builds up so intensely, I feel like I might pass out. Should we move to the bedroom? Nah. I can't stop this. I can't move myself off of him. I fumble between us until the tip of him pushes against my opening, then I wiggle forward until he's inside me. So deep, so satisfying, I might die right here at my kitchen table.

"Hey. Are you good, baby?"

I open my eyes and Adrian's examining me, my face, my eyes, like I'm the love of his life. I don't know about that, but I'm thinking he is mine. I want to tell him I love him, that I'm more than good right now, that this is all I ever wanted.

Instead, I nod and kiss him. Adrian drives deep into me, pulsing in and out until I'm on the brink. He holds back until I come. Waves of pleasure drown me until I don't know who I am, where I am, what I'm doing.

10

ADRIAN

Saturday, December 16

I wake up in Britt's bed, a smile forming on my face, until I roll over and see I'm all alone, the spot where she slept cool to the touch.

"Britt?" I sit up and swing my legs over the side, naked with a sheet covering my lap. Details from last night fill my head and I run my hand through my hair, grinning like an idiot. Where is that woman? I need her. Again.

Captain and Frappy are sitting in the doorway like marble statues, four cat eyes trained on me, only a subtle flick of Captain's tail proving they're real.

"Hello," I whisper.

They don't even blink.

A chair creaks down the hall and Britt appears in her bedroom door, hair wild from our night of incredibly hot sex, fleece pajama pants sitting low on her hips, a tank top outlining the curves of her breasts, the fabric thin enough to see her nipples. She's fucking gorgeous. My groin stirs at the sight of her.

"Cats creeping you out again?" She sips from the steaming cup of coffee in her hand as the cats purr around her calves. Her voice is husky, not yet used today.

"They're obsessed with us." I nod at the mess of sheets next to me. "Hey, come back to bed?"

But she shakes her head, and that's when I notice her furrowed brow and tight expression. It is so very unlike the expression she'd worn last night in the kitchen, or after that in the bedroom.

Uh oh. Is she freaking out? Did I misread the situation and she only needed one night to get me out of her system?

"I have a lot to do today." She's gripping her mug like it's her thin tether to life itself. "I was gonna throw on some jeans and get myself together."

"Anything I can help with? Need to decorate any school gyms, or hunt down another hundred boxes of lights?" I attempt a charming grin to melt whatever's frozen over in her since she woke up.

Nah. She's not frozen.

She's upset, or stressed, or something else negative.

It almost works, and a smile crosses her face. "Not today."

I wait for her to say more, but she stands silently in the doorway. My eyes roam over her again. She's perfect. My arms ache to pull her into them. I want to feel her skin against mine again. I want her to order me around and do dirty things to me.

"Everything okay? You're not regretting last night, are you?" It was the best night of my life. Dancing with her in the school gym, feeling like a teenager with an infatuation, then getting her home and doing what we did. My face grows warm thinking about it.

What is going through her mind?

"Of course not." She bites her bottom lip, and I want to kiss her worries away. I want to make whatever's wrong all better. I want to hear her giggle again, see her bright smile light up her face. She's covering something up. What did I do? What happened?

My gut twists. I just got her, finally let myself have her after all this time. It's not enough.

"Come here, please." I hold my hand out to her, praying she'll grasp it.

She appears to consider my request, emotions I don't understand flipping over her face like a slideshow, then moves toward me. When she gets to me, I let out a silent breath. I remove the coffee mug from her hand and slide it onto the nightstand, then pull her onto my lap. I'm hard, but I don't want to fuck her right now.

I want to love her.

Wait, what?

Oh, shit.

She relents to my touch and drapes her arm around my shoulders. I nuzzle into her neck and kiss her in the soft spot above her collarbone. Britt breathes out and melts against me, like sweet butter on a warm biscuit.

Do I love her? Have I let myself fall for this woman? Some combination of panic and joy surges through me as my lips skim her neck and she lets out another little sigh. How can it be possible?

I lean back and look into her eyes. But it *is* possible. The truth overwhelms me and my heart grows to fill my chest.

I love Britt. I'm *in* love with her.

Yeah. That's exactly right.

But I don't know how to make her pain go away. Not by telling her what I'm thinking. Not now. She doesn't want to hear it. Her eyes are already clouding over with concern.

Does she feel it too? What's between us?

I want to protect her. I want to make her feel safe and warm and loved. She's passionate and open and good, honest and determined to do the right thing. My parents hated each other, then they loved each other, then they loved other people. The fighting, the making up, the cheating. It had all been so traumatic. I never wanted to be like them.

But this? This, I want. Britt.

One night with her would never be enough.

"What are you looking at me like that for?" Britt's brow creases, but for now, she's still molded to me.

Maybe it's too much for her. Too much, too late. People think they want some intense love affair. They read romance novels and stream love stories and movies, but in reality, what they want is a boring life. The other option is just too much for most.

I should know.

"Nothing." I memorize the tilt of her head, the dark eyelashes above blue eyes. I have a dark feeling in my gut. A feeling I might not be this close to her ever again.

Did I mess up last night? This whole week? Did I screw up my chance with Britt?

She leans in to kiss me, and I'm terrified it'll be our last.

"Well." Britt breaks the kiss and hops off my lap, careful not to look down at my bare chest. "I'll grab you a coffee to go while you get dressed."

Then she disappears back out of her room, leaving both my lap and my heart chilled.

11

BRITT

Standing in my kitchen at the window, watching as Adrian backs out of my driveway, reality shifts. Was I drunk last night? Nope. I didn't have an adult beverage before the school dance, nor during, and only a few sips of wine when we got home. I was decidedly sober. Did Adrian and I have sex three times before collapsing in my bed, snuggled up together like it was the most natural thing in the world?

Yup. That one hundred percent happened. It felt perfect. Meant to be.

I drain my coffee mug and place it in the sink. He's gone from sight now, and I know what I have to do.

Last night was a fantasy.

Not just the sex. No, it was when Adrian looked at me like I was *his* fantasy. Even this morning, when he pulled me onto his lap, a sheet the only thing covering his evident desire for me.

The look on his face wasn't only that. It was more.

I woke up at five o'clock this morning, desperate for water, so I padded down to the kitchen and filled a glass. That's when I saw it. I'd left a spot in my Christmas card collage empty. Every year, I display holiday cards on my pantry door and clipped to strings on one wall in my kitchen. I always put Reese and Adrian's card front and center, eye level, so every time I open the pantry, it's their faces I see. Their gorgeous family that has come to mean so much to me.

But this year, a card from them never came.

It was my little punishment to myself, leaving that space there. I didn't expect Reese to send me a Christmas card. But that empty spot is a reminder that there's still hope. Maybe I could win her back, get the friendship I so desperately need, the one I so disastrously messed up. Am still messing up.

Last night, I was able to convince myself it was only a one-night stand with Adrian, but in the light of day, I know that's not true. The look on his face was something more.

How can I make amends with Reese after seeing him look at me like that?

And how can I be with Adrian with Reese's disapproval?

The only way to make this work is to get permission from the person least likely to give it to me.

I text Laura.

ME

Is going to talk to Reese a terrible idea?

LAURA

Um. Why would you do that?

ME

I . . . spent the night with Adrian last night

LAURA

Holy shit! Please don't go tell his ex-wife this

ME

I can't do this thing—whatever it is with Adrian—without talking to her. I need to apologize for what happened . . . for not being there for her. I don't intend to mention last night

LAURA

I don't think this is a good idea. I can't imagine she'll give you permission to be with her ex-husband. Or forgiveness

ME

Yeah. I know

LAURA

Honestly, I'd stay away from her, Britt

Dammit. She's right. I know it, but I can't take her advice. I can't stay away from Reese. My former best friend has got to understand I was doing the right thing, the best way I could. That nothing had happened. I'm not like my ex-husband.

I promised myself I'd be honest with everyone in my life. I won't share what's just happened with Adrian, but I must talk to her. I'll be mostly honest.

I dress in jeans and a sweater, then pull a brush through my hair and throw it in a familiar braid. Before I can overthink what I'm about to do, I jump in my car and drive toward Reese's new address, which I found in the online school directory.

A strong sense of déjà vu washes over me. Driving to Reese's house—a different one—to do something monumental. Layers of emotions are making my brain fuzzy. Visceral images of Adrian kissing me, nuzzling my neck, letting his hands roam over my body.

I delayed the guilt while it was happening, but this morning hit hard. I was betraying Reese, betraying myself, doing something wrong.

I hit the steering wheel with the palm of my hand as I navigate the side streets, braking too abruptly at a four-way stop sign.

What am I going to tell her? What am I asking her for? Am I truly looking for her friendship again? Would I choose that over Adrian?

I miss her so much. It's been a long six months without my best friend.

I pull into Reese's driveway, in front of a house I've never been invited into. A few months ago, she bought a modest ranch with a one-car garage. I'm sure she did okay in the divorce, but I know she makes a lot less than Adrian, so her situation must be tighter now. I cringe at the thought that it's my fault.

I shouldn't be here, but I can't stop myself from opening the car door, stepping out onto her driveway, and walking up the front steps. My hand involuntarily lifts and knocks. The door swings open and Reese appears in front of me.

Her face registers brief shock, then it clears and she crosses her arms. She's got her long hair in a braid on her shoulder, just like me. Her eyes roam over me, and I'm guessing she regrets the hairstyle.

"Hello." Her voice is steady and cool.

"I . . ." My mouth hangs open and I freeze. What do I want from her? "Reese. I miss you. So much. I'm so sorry for not being there for you. For everything." I pull in a ragged breath, trying to control my stinging tears. "Can we start over? Please? I just want to be friends again."

Even I understand the horrific contortion of me asking her for that, with her ex-husband's touch still warm on my skin. But I can only think about myself. I can only consider what I need right now, and it's loving Adrian and fixing my friendship with Reese. That's the real fantasy. Adrian in love with me. Reese as my best friend.

The fog in my head clears quite suddenly. Is this truly impossible? Those are two conflicting desires. I might not even be able to have *one* of those.

But I can't have both.

Unless I fight for it, really hard.

Her cat peeks out from behind her legs.

"Hi, Peanut Butter," I say with a shaky voice. While Reese

assesses me with narrowed eyes, I squat down and pet her cat's head, almost as familiar to me as Captain and Frappy.

"Get back inside, kitty." Without looking down, Reese waves her foot until Peanut Butter trots back to where he came from. Reese's face is stony. "You had feelings for my husband. You can't do that and expect forgiveness."

I wait for her to say more, but she's biting her cheek to stop herself. There's some kind of emotion there, but it's not just hate, I'm sure of it.

"I'm so sorry, Reese." Here is where I should say it wasn't real, that there were no feelings. But it's not true. "Is there any way I can earn your friendship back?" I lift my hands to her, palms up, offering my heart. "I know it wouldn't be the same, but maybe . . ."

"I don't think so." Reese cuts me off and squints her eyes shut. What's she thinking? Counting down to stay calm? Thinking of ways to murder me? "The divorce is final."

"Ree . . ."

She opens her eyes. "So I guess you're free to be with Adrian, if you still want him. I heard you had a moment together last night at the dance."

I flinch and step back. Did Chelsea see and tell her? Or maybe Reese is a friend of Liz's or one of the other moms. Did they see us behind the curtain? In the basement? Or could they just tell by the way Adrian and I looked at each other?

God, I'm the worst.

But did Reese just technically give me permission to be with Adrian?

"I just—" I can't deny it. I can't pretend that I wasn't tangled with her ex-husband last night and sitting on his lap in my bed just thirty minutes ago.

Reese stares, pressing her lips together, searching my face, and for a split second, I imagine the way she used to look at me when we were best friends. But now, she sees right through me.

"Go home, Britt."

"I'm so sorry," I whisper. "Maybe over time?"

In response, Reese simply closes the door gently in my face, leaving me alone on her front steps, more confused than ever.

12

ADRIAN

There's been no word from Britt since I left her house this morning.

ME

> Last night was amazing. I think we over-delivered at the winter dance

My attempt at a joke gets no response, so an hour later, I try again.

ME

> Thanks for letting me stay over last night. Can I see you later?

But as soon as I send it, I know it's too casual. Too flippant. Something's going on with Britt, and I can only hope she lets me back in. Because maybe I can help her work it out.

When she doesn't respond for two more hours, I send another, because I'm desperate, apparently, or maybe just in love.

ME

> Hey. Are you okay?

I should have said something different. My text implies something is wrong, and maybe nothing is. Maybe I should've told her how beautiful she is, or how much I don't regret last night, or how much I want to kiss her again.

Was last night a mistake? Not for me. No way. But what if it was for Britt? The look on her face this morning was full of complex layers of emotion, and not all of them good. And the way she wants to be friends with Reese? *Shit.*

I want to help her get everything she dreams of, but that might be too much.

I stand in the toiletries aisle at the pharmacy. Britt's family room was fully decorated for Christmas, complete with a beautiful tree and stockings lining the mantel. One for her, Jackson, and each of her cats.

That's when I realized I don't have a stocking—or stocking stuffers—for Chelsea.

So far, I've added some apple-scented hand lotion, a loofah, nail polish, and an app store gift card to my basket. Will she like any of these things? Probably not, but then, I'm pretty sure that she won't like anything coming from me. The girl will be forever mad at me for this divorce. And it'll get even worse if I keep seeing Britt. That look on Chelsea's face as she watched us in the gym last night wasn't a good one.

A cold tendril of despair weaves itself around my insides. Shitty husband, shitty father, shitty friend, and shitty, well, whatever I am to Britt.

And I don't even have an actual stocking for my daughter. I grit my teeth. If I can help Britt find one hundred boxes of lights, I can find a stocking for Chelsea and stuff it until it explodes.

I leave the aisle and head over to the Christmas decorations, which are mostly picked over, except for a shelf full of gross-sounding flavored candy canes, like hot tamale and sour apple. I grab some for Chelsea's stocking.

That's when I spot it. My feet freeze in place and I stare at the single box of fairy lights on the shelf.

I pick it up and turn it over in my hands, remembering the laughing fit Britt and I had on Wednesday at store number, what? Three? Four? A smile crosses my face and stays there, refusing to be bullied by my previous negative thoughts.

I snap a photo and send it to Britt.

ME

Need another box of lights?

There's nothing in response.

I wish I knew what she was thinking. That I could tell her what I am thinking.

I wish I could tell her I love her.

I close my eyes and breathe in through my nose. What is holding me back? I'd upset my ex-wife. I'd upset my daughter. I'd feel like a bad person.

Seriously good reasons, actually.

But those things are all happening anyway. Should I punish myself forever for the mistakes I made in my marriage? Is that how it's supposed to work? Maybe it is, but it doesn't feel right. Last night, this week, all those hours spent with Britt. That felt right. Good. Pure. Not wrong.

Nothing happened with Britt while I was married. I didn't know she had feelings for me. I didn't let myself consider falling for her, not on any kind of conscious level.

But now, I'm divorced. And I need to figure out a way to live the rest of my life. Could I make it work with Britt? Even if some people would hate it?

I could talk to Chelsea. Convince her of how much I love her and that I'll do everything I can to be the best father possible.

I could talk to Reese. Tell her about me and Britt. Do it in a way that makes her feel like a friend. Is it possible? I don't think so, but at least I can remove volatility—which infiltrated all of my parents' interactions—from the conversation. Maybe it wouldn't have been as bad if my folks had been able to keep their emotions under control and just dealt with the reality of their situation. Maybe they would have divorced years earlier and kept things civil.

Maybe Reese and I could do that.

I'm sure she hates me right now, but maybe over time, we can develop a better relationship. Be the best co-parents we can. Maybe even be friends, like Britt so desperately wants.

My phone buzzes in my hand.

BRITT

I think we're good with lights

No smiley face, no heart emoji, nothing. I need to talk to her in person. I want to tell her I love her.

That I'm in love with her.

ME

Can I see you tonight?

BRITT

I can't. I have Jackson and we're doing movie night

ME

Tomorrow?

BRITT

We have lunch plans at noon with my parents

ME

How about after that?

BRITT

I don't know. Maybe. We should probably talk

Uh oh.

She's planning a way to cut me out of her life. Maybe even hoping I'll disappear on my own. But that isn't going to happen. I know she still has feelings for me. I could see it in her eyes, even though I could also see she's not going to let herself fall. I'm going to have to think of a way to win her over. Will she try to break things off with me? My insides twist. Probably.

But that just means I have to fight for her.

I move a few feet down the aisle and scan the remaining stockings, most of which have cartoon characters on them. That will not fly with my daughter. I push aside the dogs from Paw Patrol, the crew from Mickey Mouse, and other characters I don't recognize.

But then I spot it. Like the box of lights in my basket, there's just one left on the shelf. I grab the red fuzzy stocking and add it to my shopping basket. I got lucky.

Maybe I'll get lucky with Britt, too.

13

———

BRITT

Sunday, December 17

I glance at Jackson in the rearview mirror as we pull away from the Italian restaurant. My parents are leaving for a week to a Caribbean island over Christmas, so we had our celebration with them early.

It would never occur to them to invite me and Jackson to join them on vacation, let alone host us in their house. Or even accept an invitation to share the holiday at ours.

Not that I've offered in years.

I wish my brother could've joined us today, but he resolutely avoids our parents. Then again, he doesn't need to try very hard on that front. They spent little time with us growing up, so it's unsurprising, if not disappointing, that they don't spend much time with us now.

I was thrilled when Jackson's friend's mom texted me this morning, inviting him to their house this afternoon. It was the perfect excuse to have a firm end time for lunch. We didn't even have dessert.

"You okay, buddy?"

My son doesn't look up from the fidget spinner in his hands. "Yup."

"That was a cool LEGO set they bought you for Christmas, huh? It was a huge one."

"Yeah, it was fine. I wish they had gotten Minecraft, though. Or Jurassic World. Not the boring City one."

"Jackson." My mouth quirks on one side, and I can't seem to chastise him further for not being thankful for the gift. "Well. We can exchange it if you'd like. They taped the gift receipt on the box. I bet you can find another you like better."

"Thanks, Mom." He's silent for a few minutes. "Were they always so boring?"

I let out a short laugh. "What do you mean?"

"I mean, when you were growing up, what was it like?"

Yeah, boring. I press my lips together and paste a fake smile on my face.

"Well, it was me and your uncle, and a staff of au pairs and nannies." I chuckle, but there's no humor in the sound. "Grandma and Grandpa didn't do a lot with us. They traveled all the time for Grandpa's work, and Grandma was always busy organizing fundraisers for charities. They didn't involve us in any of that. So yeah, it was a bit of a quiet house. But I made my own fun." I steal another peek back at him, still staring out the window.

"I'm glad *you're* more fun," he states matter-of-factly. "Sometimes I wish there was more going on in our house. Alex has, like, three sisters. Did you know that?"

I sigh and swallow the small lump popping up in my throat. "Yeah, buddy, I know. But would you want to have three sisters messing with all your LEGO sets?" I attempt to insert levity in my voice.

"I mean, whenever I'm there, someone's fighting or crying or in trouble, so I guess that's not great."

"We have a good time, right?" I try so hard for Jackson. It's why I left my corporate job to make sure I'm home and around whenever he needs me. It's why I cared so much about the dance—not only because he misses Chelsea. I always think about decorating the Christmas tree just right, getting the stockings up, doing all the holiday things to create a warm, loving place for him to call home.

But it never feels like enough.

"Yeah." He nods and meets my eyes in the rearview mirror. "The dance was fun. I really liked that."

"Good. I'm glad. We tried to make it special for you kids."

He's silent for another ten minutes and I turn on a playlist from my phone for background noise. More children would have been amazing. I would've loved to have a big, loud house with people everywhere. Never alone, never lonely, always exciting.

"Mom?"

"Yeah, dude?"

"Are you gonna have more babies?"

Well, shit.

I let out a squeaky laugh. "Oh, man. I'm not sure, Jackson."

It's possible. I'm only thirty-two. But to open my heart up like that again to a man and a baby? I can't picture it.

Kids. I let out a rush of air. They have a way of poking their salt-covered fingers in the raw wounds of your biggest insecurities.

"Okay." The fidget spinner clicks as it rotates.

But then a fully formed vision springs up in my mind. One of Adrian and me living in my house, Jackson in his room, Chelsea taking the guest room as her own, and my study converted to a nursery. I picture Adrian dancing with me in the kitchen, his hand steadying my pregnant belly, music on in the background, kids laughing, joy filling every corner of the house.

Isn't there a way for it to work? For me and Adrian to be together? My stomach tightens into knots strong enough to secure a cruise ship.

Couldn't we all co-parent together?

I pull to a stop in Jackson's friend's driveway.

"Bye, Mom!" He flings himself out of the car and I roll down my window, my insides swirling with the gorgeous vision.

"I'll pick you up in a few hours." I wave to Alex's mom and back up onto the street.

I need to get home to think, to get that vision out of my head. But it's sticky. It grows and becomes clearer as I get closer to home.

Should I deny myself that joy if there's even a tiny chance of it happening? But would I be able to live with myself? Forgive myself for screwing up my friendship with Reese? Could I let it go?

I turn into my driveway, only noticing Adrian's SUV at the last moment.

14

ADRIAN

Oh, fuck, she's here. I peek out through the blinds of the Idea Garage as Britt's car turns into the driveway.

Please don't let her think I've crossed the line. Please don't let this be a giant mistake.

But it isn't. It can't be. Even if she rejects me, I'm just being true to my feelings and embracing the passion I feel for her. It's not all bad and destructive. I love this woman, and I plan on laying it all out in front of her. I'm going to offer her everything I have.

And if I fail? At least I tried.

Britt brakes when she sees my SUV in her driveway. There's no backing out now. I look around and stifle a nervous chuckle.

I went Over. The. Top.

She can literally have me arrested for trespassing.

I waited until after I knew she'd be gone to lunch with her parents and Jackson, then let myself in with the garage code. I dragged the bins of lights from the winter dance into the Idea Garage and got to work. Frappy and Captain were curious, at one point settling into one of the empty containers to watch me decorate.

Maybe they don't hate me after all.

Britt gets out of her car and stares at my SUV. I send her the text I have ready.

ME

> Come to the Idea Garage. I have a surprise for you

She grabs her phone from her pocket and reads it, then glances up, making direct eye contact with me as I peek through her blinds. *Shit.* That probably makes me look like a real stalker. I'll have to make it up to her right away.

I step back and wait for her to come inside. It takes a hundred years for the knob to turn and the door to slowly open.

Britt steps inside. "Adrian?" Then she gasps, her hand flying to her chest.

I've strung up about half of the school dance white fairy lights. I would've done more, but there was no more room. I lined the walls—careful to use hooks that wouldn't damage the walls or paint when I take it all down—doorways, tables, desks, the loft area, and the kitchen. The dark December day helps, since no sun streams in from the windows and the effect is a holiday wonderland.

Britt wanders to the center of the room, her mouth parted, eyes flitting everywhere, resting for a beat on the kitchen table, where there's a chilled bottle of champagne and two flutes.

If this doesn't work out, it'll get awkward real fast in here.

"Britt." I savor the sound of her name on my lips.

She squeaks and slips off her jacket, throwing it on the couch and spinning in a slow circle, eyes wide. "What did you do?"

Something right, that's for sure, because she has an awestruck smile as she turns.

"I decorated. You taught me everything I needed to know about making a place magical with strings of lights."

She giggles and stops spinning.

"And—" I take a step toward her. "The thing is, I've been dying to dance with you again."

"You want to dance with me? Here?" She rubs her arms and then slides her hands on either side of her neck, as if she needs grounding—a reminder she's here, and something big is happening.

"Better than the high school gym, no?"

"At least we don't have to hide behind curtains." Britt makes a sound I can't place, something that makes me think her body is humming in response to mine, wanting to touch me as much as I want to touch her. She looked hot as hell on Friday night, but she's just as gorgeous today in jeans and a thin, gray sweater.

"So? Will you dance with me?" I hold out my hand.

Britt nods. Then she does the best thing I can imagine—she places her hand in mine.

"Alexa, play the song."

Britt's mouth quirks up as the familiar slow guitar strums fill the air. "Is this the song we danced to on Friday?"

"Yeah, I think it's ours now."

She smiles again, and I can see the joy reflected in her eyes.

I pull her body against mine, arms wrapped around her waist. Her hands press against my chest, her eyes fixed on mine. Oh, this is right. This is exactly how it should be.

"Adrian," she whispers and presses her lips together. But she says nothing else.

That's fine, because there's something I have to say first.

I splay my hand on her back, feeling the warmth of her body as we sway together, my chest filling with its own warmth.

"Six months ago, I was an idiot."

She blinks. "No, I was. Not you. I shouldn't have made such a big deal of things. I should've just . . ."

"Hush, baby, let me get through this." I touch my finger to her lips, then gliding it down the curve of her neck, her shoulder, and grabbing her hand again. "I'd closed myself off so tight, blind to what was growing between us. You weren't imagining it. You weren't alone. I was just too stupid to realize what was happening."

I take a deep breath, grounding myself in the moment.

"But you, Britt. You were so brave. You saw it when I didn't. You tried to do the right thing. I know that."

She chuckles and blows out air. "Maybe I should try harder in the future."

I want to kiss her so badly, and my eyes drift to her lips. But it's not time. Not quite yet. "That's one of the things that makes you so incredible. And I have to tell you—I *need* to tell you—that I'm absolutely, completely, and overwhelmingly in love with you."

Britt takes a sharp breath.

"I'll do anything to be with you. Anything." I rub the inside of her wrist with my thumb. The other hand remains on her back. I won't let her go. Not until she tells me to get out.

This is where I belong. With her.

"I know there are complications. But we can overcome anything together. You and me."

"Oh, god, Adrian." Tears fill her eyes and her hand is shaking in mine. She's not letting me go, either. "I don't know. I don't know . . ."

"We can light up a whole school gym by sheer will and determination." I touch my finger under her chin and tilt her face up to me, placing my lips on hers for a brief kiss. I can't resist. "You're worthy of the most true and deep love out there. I will give it to you. I will give you anything and everything. Just tell me you're willing to let me spoil you every single day."

Her cheeks flush and I can see the switch in her face when it clicks.

"I've just done it all wrong," she whimpers, but her body melts into mine, as if we are one person instead of two.

"No." I kiss her again, this time for longer, with the slightest flicker of my tongue inside her mouth. "You've done it your way. Now we can do it our way. Together."

Britt throws her other arm around my neck and drags me down to kiss her again and again.

Breathless, I pull away. "Did you get that I'm madly in love with you?"

She nods, her eyes flicking to my lips and back again. "I love you too. I've loved you for a long time. And now you've done this." She looks around, eyes wide, an open smile lighting up her face along with the lights.

We kiss again, and this time, when I look up to see her cats supervising, it feels like we're doing everything right.

15

BRITT

Sunday, December 24

This is the first year since my divorce that I haven't had Jackson on Christmas Eve. In the past, we'd always spend the holiday with Reese, Adrian, and Chelsea. But not this year.

I'd been dreading it.

So back in the fall, when Jackson's dad requested we switch holidays, I agreed. After all, our December 24 would be very different than what Jackson is used to.

And it is different. Wonderfully different.

Adrian's also alone this year, since Chelsea is spending the holiday with her mother. He sits next to me on my couch, an open bottle of wine on the coffee table in front of us, a fire burning in the electric fireplace next to my towering tree, our hands linked. There are no screens, no distractions. Only each other.

Oh, and soft cats curled on either side of us.

It's been a week since he decked out the Idea Garage with way too many lights. A week since he confessed his love. I've accepted that I can let myself love him, be with him, and that it's okay that this didn't start out the right way.

"I can't believe you talked to Reese and Chelsea about us," I murmur, squeezing his hand. "And that it went so badly."

"She really went off on me, which is so not like Reese."

"And Chelsea walking in during the fight?" I groan. "Such bad timing."

"The worst timing."

"Do you regret telling them?"

Adrian shakes his head firmly. "No. I didn't want them speculating or finding out another way. Chelsea told Reese that she'd seen us together at the dance, so Reese already suspected something was going on. For real, this time."

I press my lips together. The happiness I feel with Adrian right now is tempered by the confirmation that Reese knows everything and is furious all over again. I sigh deeply and lean my head on his shoulder, relishing the way our bodies fit together. Perfectly. As if we were made for each other.

"Still, it was brave of you to be honest."

"Well. They hate me. But I'm going to work on it, and not hide anything anymore. I want to be honest with you, with Reese, and with Chelsea. I'm going to work every day to prove to Chelsea how much she means to me. If it means I have to plan every school dance or befriend scary PTO moms, I'll do it."

"You're a good dad, like I keep telling you. She'll come around." I pause for a beat. "And I want to be friends with Reese. Is that crazy?"

It's Adrian's turn to groan. He kisses my hand, gazing at me with eyes full of love. I know that now.

"After all this? You're trying to save your friendship? The ex-wife of the man you're in love with?"

Butterflies flutter in my stomach. This is man I'm in love with. And for him to love me back? It's everything.

"Well, when you say it like that, it sounds ridiculous."

"It *is* ridiculous." He slowly moves his head back and forth.

"You're amazing. You still care so much about what she thinks. It's going to be really hard, Britt."

"Think I have a chance?"

"No, not really, but if you want to try, I'm behind you. I wasn't a good husband, but I can be a better co-parent. Reese will pull it together. For Chelsea. I know she will." Adrian runs his free hand up and down my thigh. "But I think if we are kind and open over time, we'll eventually win her over."

I bite my bottom lip. "We'll wear her down with kindness?"

He nods and grabs our wine glasses, handing me mine before leaning back against the couch, relaxing into me again. I snuggle in as close as possible without climbing into his lap.

"So you'll try to be friends with your ex-wife?" I sip from my wine glass, enjoying the warmth filling my belly and the happiness in my chest, trying to let go of the uncomfortable feelings I have about Reese.

Adrian grunts. "I'm not sure about friends. But I'll try. You've inspired me to be a better person, Britt. I believe I can do that with you. So yeah, I'm up for it."

"That makes me happy."

He sips his wine and turns his head to me. "That's all I want. But Britt?"

"Yes?"

"Can we stop talking about all of that?"

I nod and drink from my glass before leaning forward to deposit it on the table. It's been at least ten minutes since this man kissed me.

I move forward and pause right before pressing my lips against his.

"I know something that will distract me." I run my hands from his pecs to right below the top of his jeans, pausing there as I close the gap between our mouths.

After a long, sweet kiss, Adrian puts his drink aside and uses both hands to pull me onto his lap. Welp, there we go.

"This is my favorite Christmas Eve ever," he murmurs, burying his face in my neck.

I breathe out and wiggle against him, loving the moan that escapes his throat.

"Me too."

I can't wait to see what the future holds for us.

THE END

Enjoyed *One Hundred Lights*? Leave a review, it helps spread the word. And good news—*One Hundred Lights* is a prequel novella! Read about Reese and her sisters in the completed Hart Sisters Trilogy. Just be prepared to hate Britt & Adrian a little (okay, a lot) in Reese's story. Don't get too mad at me!

If We Pretend is Reese & Oliver's love story. It's a fake dating, divorced mom, ex pro soccer player light sports romance set in Scotland.

Unless It's You is Stella & Ethan's love story. Set in London, this romance is a second chance, enemies-to-lovers, bucket list novel.

Since We're Here is Maddie & Patrick's love story. It's a grumpy sunshine Irish romance.

Stay in touch:
Instagram: @ChrissyHopewell
Facebook: ChrissyHopewellAuthor
TikTok: @ChrissyHopewellBooks
Email: Chrissy@ChrissyHopewell.com

Free content, including bonus chapters for each novel:
www.ChrissyHopewell.com

if we
PRETEND
a fake dating Scottish romance
FAKE DATING IS
MORE REAL
IN SCOTLAND
CHRISSY HOPEWELL

UNLESS *it's you*

CHRISSY HOPEWELL

SINCE we're here

a grumpy sunshine Irish romance

SHE BRINGS
THE SUNSHINE
TO IRELAND.

CHRISSY HOPEWELL

ACKNOWLEDGMENTS

I'll keep this short and sweet, just like this novella (except for that one scene that's more spicy than sweet). Writing a book is a solitary activity, but you can't do it alone. I'm so lucky to have a fantastic writing community filled with supportive humans, especially Hannah, Lillian, Roma, Lisa, Bella, Gabriella, Natalie and Paris. And so many more from my Pitch Wars class! Thank you to beta readers and early CPs of *One Hundred Lights*, including Ericka, Cate, Lisa, Lillian, and my editor, Brenda Chin. So many people encourage me on my writing journey! My besties from high school: Ericka, Cate, Allison, and Wendy; my husband, Jason, and our four children who mostly put up with me disappearing with my laptop to write or edit. If you are reading this, thank YOU so much for picking up a Chrissy Hopewell story! I hope you loved it. There's so much more to come from me!

Love, Chrissy

ABOUT THE AUTHOR

Chrissy Hopewell started her love for romance novels by sneaking her mom's steamy books in middle school. She has spent varying amounts of time overseas, including working at a pub in Dublin, waitressing at a hotel in the Scottish Borders, and studying and living in London. Because of these experiences, international flair and accents often show up in her writing. Chrissy now lives in the suburbs of Cincinnati, Ohio with her family, and she no longer has to sneak what she reads.

instagram.com/chrissyhopewell

tiktok.com/@chrissyhopewellbooks

facebook.com/chrissyhopewellauthor